GW01229998

The Analog Sea Review

NUMBER THREE

THE ANALOG SEA REVIEW · NUMBER THREE

Copyright © 2020 Analog Sea

The acknowledgments on pp. 216–218 constitute
an extension of this copyright page.

All rights reserved. No part of this work may be used or
reproduced in any manner whatsoever without written
permission from the publisher except in the case of brief
quotations embodied in critical articles and reviews.

Printed in Germany

Published by Analog Sea
PO Box 11670
Austin, Texas 78711
United States

Basler Strasse 115
79115 Freiburg
Germany

Editors Jonathan S. Simons,
Janos Tedeschi, and Elena Fritz

Cover Artwork
Joseph-Antoine d'Ornano

ISBN 978-1-7322519-7-7

The Analog Sea Review
Number Three

AN OFFLINE MANIFESTO *Jonathan Simons*	1
GIRL IN GREEN DRESS *Sally Rosenbaum*	4
LITERATURE CONTAINS ALL ART *Gaston Bachelard*	5
IN THE PRESENCE OF REALITY *Virginia Woolf*	7
ETERNAL INK *Anne Fadiman*	8
ON QUALITY *Peter Brook*	15
THE ETERNAL SECRET *Stefan Zweig*	17
MUST I CREATE? *Rainer Maria Rilke*	20
THE FORGING *Jorge Luis Borges*	23
RAILROAD SUNSET *Edward Hopper*	24
INTERVIEW WITH WIM WENDERS *Jonathan Simons*	25
ALICE IN THE CITIES *Wim Wenders*	43
SMASHING THE TELEVISION *Alexander Graf*	44
THE OLD MASTER JOHN FORD *Harry Tomicek*	47
THE LOST WORLD *Siegfried Schober*	49
A LANGUAGE OF IMAGES *Wim Wenders*	51
THE PHOTOGRAPHIC EXPERIENCE *Susan Sontag*	52
ONCE *Jonathan Simons*	53
TAUFROST *Fritz von Wille*	54

NUMBER THREE

ADAGISSIMO *Leonard Bernstein*		55
THE NORTH AS ARCHETYPE *Howard Fink*		62
THE IDEA OF NORTH *Glenn Gould*		69
SILENCE AND SOLITUDE *Blaise Pascal*		79
THE BEHAVIOR OF LIGHT *Barry Lopez*		80
ROTTEN ICE *Gretel Ehrlich*		82
WUNDERKAMMER *Ralph Waldo Emerson*		83
THE LOST PIANOS OF SIBERIA *Sophy Roberts*		84
YOU AND ART *William Stafford*		87
ADVICE TO A GRADUATION *Glenn Gould*		88
AT THE BLUE NOTE *Pablo Medina*		97
MUSIKANT AUF DEM HEIMWEG *Hugo Mühlig*		98
TANGIER SYNDROME *Simon-Pierre Hamelin*		99
POETAS DEL MUNDO *Jonathan Davidson*		109
WHERE ARE THE INTELLECTUALS? *Alberto Manguel*		118
IN DARK TIMES *Bertolt Brecht*		125
THE VIENNA OF YESTERDAY *George Prochnik*		126
SAVING VIENNA *Stefan Zweig*		129
LIGHT FOR A COLD LAND *Arthur Erickson*		130
THIS HEAVY CRAFT *P. K. Page*		133
UNTITLED *C. G. Jung*		134

THE ANALOG SEA REVIEW

WHERE IT ALL BEGAN *C. G. Jung*	135
INTERVIEW WITH ANDRÉS OCAZIONEZ *Jonathan Simons*	136
CONFRONTATION WITH THE UNCONSCIOUS *C. G. Jung*	147
THE DISENCHANTMENT OF THE WORLD *Morris Berman*	149
TOWARD INDIVIDUATION *C. G. Jung*	154
INTERVIEW WITH WOLFGANG GIEGERICH *Jonathan Simons*	156
IKIGAI *Jeremy Page*	169
ALICE *Emil Nolde*	170
JOURNAL OF A SOLITUDE *May Sarton*	171
WHAT IS DIFFICULT *Rainer Maria Rilke*	174
A ROOM AT THE BACK *Patrick Curry*	175
THE MAN IN HIS TOWER *Kenneth Clark*	180
REMAINING ONESELF *Stefan Zweig*	183
THAT STROKE OF THE LIGHTHOUSE *Virginia Woolf*	188
LETTERS FROM SHENANDOAH *Jean James*	190
KINGFISHER *Jackie Morris*	192
SILT *Robert Macfarlane*	193
SPINNING STORIES *David Abram*	199
IN SEARCH OF DARKNESS *Maria Browning*	201
NEWGRANGE *Thomas R. Smith*	206
TO LIVE WISELY *Barry Lopez*	208

NUMBER THREE

EVERY MORNING ALL OVER AGAIN *William Stafford*	209
SUMMER APEX *Peter Huntoon*	210
ARTWORK	212
CONTRIBUTORS	213
ACKNOWLEDGMENTS	216

An Offline Manifesto
Jonathan Simons

From the Editor

Although creative tools and publication have never been more accessible, the conditions an artist needs to develop vision and skill are disappearing. A person never left alone for any length of time, never left to fumble in the dark for their own voice, develops little more than a passion for retweeting the chatter and opinions of others. Art demands interiority.

With its promises of endless amusement and togetherness, digital utopianism continues to pull us deeper into dark waters. How far will we go? How much of our lives and culture will we hand over to our new digital overlords? And if we tell the network everything, holding back nothing precious or unformed, what prevents us from trusting the network more than we trust ourselves? What need then for privacy at all?

This quest for seamless connection to the Internet continues to drive engineering. The smartphone is a dinosaurian device compared to future invisible interfaces designed to keep us effortlessly linked to the network at all times. And while constant connectivity may represent the pinnacle of progress for governments and corporations, how will it shape the arts and letters? We continue to associate innovation and genius with *free thinking*, but where is this freedom when the crowd is always watching us, when our every click is surveilled, when our thoughts and emotions are puppeteered by algorithms which know us better than we know ourselves? Democracies are defined by those who fight for freedom. This is why the revolution will not be digitized.

It was once clearer where the marketplace ended and our personal lives began. While history knows authoritarianism well, there was a time when the idea of total corporate domination remained the stuff of conspiracy theory and science fiction. Even in the throes of late capitalism, we assumed the reach of the free market had its limits. Never could we have imagined that the marketplace would eventually penetrate every corner of our lives, from our homes and universities to our hallowed museums and libraries, our park benches and sidewalks, our forests, and even the open ocean. How difficult it has become to escape the cold arms of trade.

Right now, millions of people are confessing to their gadgets their loneliness, or their fear of dying, and the gadgets are responding with music and discounts. We are beyond the threshold of absurdity. At this critical moment, we must identify what of our lives and culture should remain offline, untethered from pernicious groupthink and untouched by the philistine disruptions of big-tech capital.

Several years ago, my coeditors and I decided to establish Analog Sea as an offline publishing house and institute. We advocate for the human right to disconnect. The Internet is a spectacular tool, but we believe that *offline culture* is indispensable. Preserving the printed word is of great significance, along with the physical spaces where humans look other humans in the eye, where civil dialogue and undivided attention are privileged, and where thoughts and imagination have space to meander and roam. These are life-sustaining countermeasures to the pixelated madness overtaking our world. More than faceless friends and viral memes, we urgently need thriving human communities.

Our work at Analog Sea is a search-and-rescue mission for a special kind of individual, endangered yet essential should we wish to preserve truth and beauty through another dark age. We seek out and cultivate those for whom the roots of life remain firmly planted in the real world, unfettered by the Internet and its incessant drip of spectacle and noise. We want to inspire the artists, writers, and philosophers who maintain our collective ability to dream. A society unable to dream lacks the imagination to know what freedom looks like. Eliminate the dreamers and we fall too easily for fascism and war. How desperately we need the strength to dream and the artists and thinkers to show us how.

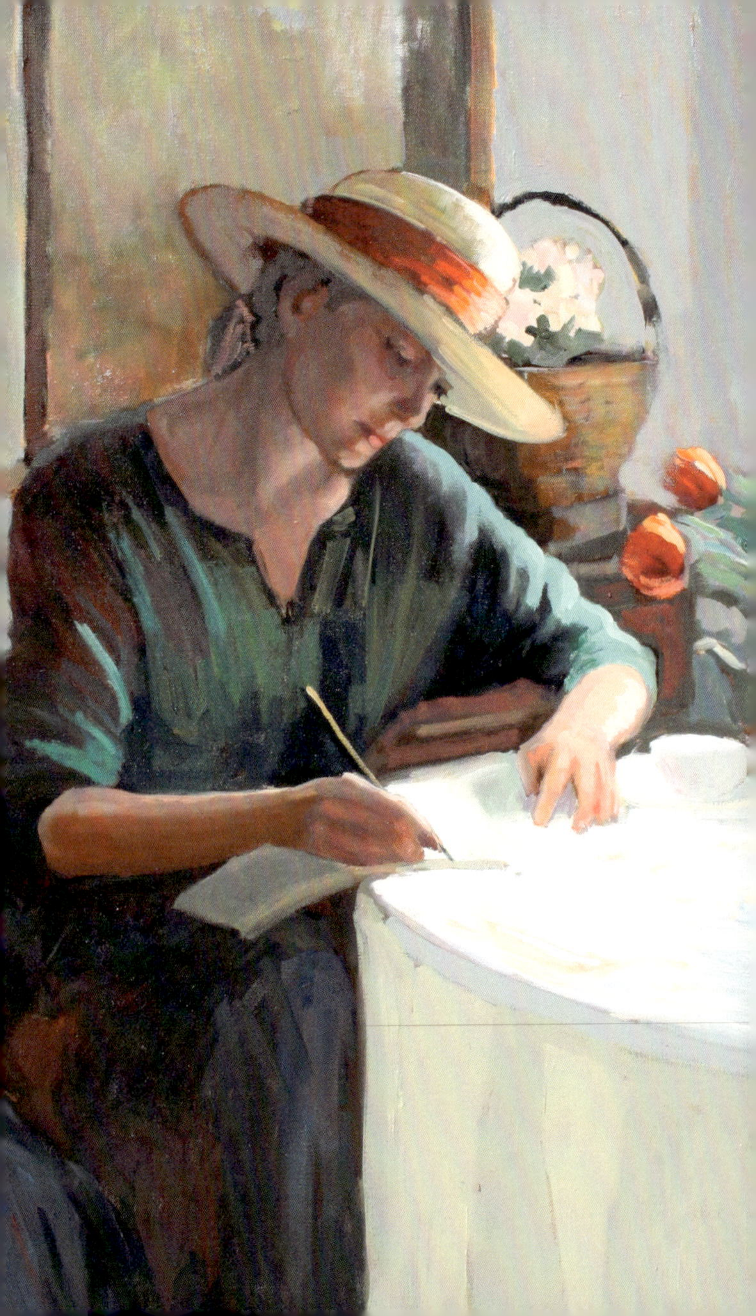

Literature Contains All Art
Gaston Bachelard

It has often been said that the child contains all possibilities. As children, we were painters, modelers, botanists, sculptors, architects, hunters, explorers. What has become of all that?

At the very heart of maturity, however, there is a means of regaining these lost possibilities. A means? What! I might be a great painter?—Yes, you might be a great painter a few hours a day.—I might create masterworks?—Yes, you might create wonderful masterworks, works that would give *you* the direct joys of wonderment, which would take you back to the happy time when the world was a source of wonder.

That means is literature. One has but to *write* the painted work. One has but to write the statue. Pen in hand—if only we are willing to be sincere—we regain all the powers of youth, we reëxperience these powers as they used to be, in their naïve assurance, with their rapid, linear, sure joys. Through the channel of *literary imagination*, all the arts are ours. A beautiful adjective, well placed, in the right light, sounding in the proper harmony of vowels, is all we need for a substance. A stylistic trait is enough for a personality, for a man. Speaking, writing! Telling, narrating! Inventing the past! Remembering, pen in hand, with the acknowledged and evident intention *to write well*, *to compose*, *to make beautiful*, in order to be quite sure that we go beyond the autobiography of a real past event and that we rediscover the autobiography of lost possibilities, the very dreams, the true, real dreams, which we lived with slow, lingering pleasure. The specific aesthetics of literature is to be found there. Literature functions as a substitute. It restores life to lost possibilities.

Excerpted from Gaston Bachelard, *On Poetic Imagination and Reverie*, trans. Colette Gaudin (Putnam, CT: Spring Publications, Inc., 2014), pp. 154–155. First published in 1971.

In the Presence of Reality
Virginia Woolf

What is meant by *reality*? It would seem to be something very erratic, very undependable—now to be found in a dusty road, now in a scrap of newspaper in the street, now a daffodil in the sun. It lights up a group in a room and stamps some casual saying. It overwhelms one walking home beneath the stars and makes the silent world more real than the world of speech—and then there it is again in an omnibus in the uproar of Piccadilly. Sometimes, too, it seems to dwell in shapes too far away for us to discern what their nature is. But whatever it touches, it fixes and makes permanent. This is what remains over when the skin of the day has been cast into the hedge; that is what is left of past time and of our loves and hates. Now the writer, as I think, has the chance to live more than other people in the presence of this reality. It is his business to find it and collect it and communicate it to the rest of us.

Excerpted from Virginia Woolf, *A Room of One's Own* (London: Penguin Classics, 2019), p. 90. First published in 1929.

Eternal Ink
Anne Fadiman

Thirty-three years ago, when I first laid eyes on it, my pen was already old. The barrel was a blue so uningratiatingly somber that in most lights it looked black. The cap, weathered from silver to gunmetal, had almost invisibly fine longitudinal striations and an opalescent ferrule that I imagined to be a precious jewel. The clip was gold and shaped like an arrow. To fill the pen, you unscrewed the last inch of barrel, submerged the nib in ink, and depressed a translucent plastic plunger—a sensuous advance over my previous pen's flaccid ink bladder, which made rude noises when it was squeezed.

My pen was a gift from my fifth-grade boyfriend, Jeffrey Davison, a freckled redhead who excelled at spelling bees and handball: the prototype of all the smart jocks I would fall for over the years, culminating in my husband. I have the feeling Jeffrey stole it from his stepfather, but no matter. The pen was mine by virtue of Jeffrey's love and by divine right. No one could have cherished it, for both its provenance and its attributes, more than I. Until I was in college, I reserved it for poetry—prose would have profaned it—and later, during my beginning years as a writer, I used it for every first draft. Like a dog that needs to circle three times before settling down to sleep, I could not write an opening sentence until I had uncapped the bottle of India ink, inhaled the narcotic fragrance of carbon soot and resin, dipped the nib, and pumped the plunger—one, two, three, four, five.

Muses are fickle, and many a writer, peering into the void, has escaped paralysis by ascribing the creative responsibility to a talisman: a lucky charm, a brand of paper, but most often a writing instrument. Am I writing well? Thank my pen. Am I writing badly? Don't blame me, blame my pen. By such displacements does the fearful imagination defend itself. During one dry period, Virginia Woolf wrote, "I am writing with a pen which is feeble and wispy"; during another, "What am I going to say with a defective nib?" Goethe, although he had learned elegant penmanship from a *magister artis scribendi*, dictated his great works to a copyist. This scriptorial remove only intensified his need to control the rituals of composition. He insisted that the quills be cut neither too long nor too short; that the feather plumes be removed; that the freshly inked pages be dried in front of the stove and not with sand; and that all of the above be done noiselessly, lest his concentration be broken.

Kipling was incapable of writing fiction with a pencil. Only ink would do, the blacker the better ("all 'blue-blacks' were an abomination to my Daemon"). His favorite pen, with which he wrote *Plain Tales* in Lahore, was "a slim, octagonal-sided, agate penholder with a Waverley nib." It snapped one day, and although it was followed by a succession of dip pens, fountain pens, and pump pens, Kipling regarded these as "impersonal hirelings" and spent the rest of his life mourning the deceased Waverley.

I know how Kipling felt. Pen-bereavement is a serious matter. Ten years ago, my pen disappeared into thin air. Like a jealous lover, I never took it out of the house, so I have always believed that in rebellion against its purdah it rolled into a hidden crack in my desk. A thousand times have I been tempted to tear the desk apart; a thousand times have I resisted, fearing that the pen would not be there after all and that I would be forced to admit it was gone forever. For a time I haunted shops that sold secondhand pens, pathetically clutching an old writing sample and saying, "This is the width of the line I want." I might as well have carried a photograph of a dead lover and said, "Find me another just like this." Along the way I learned that my pen had been a Parker 51, circa 1945. Eventually I found one that matched mine not only in vintage but in color. But after this parvenu came home with me, it swung wantonly from scratching to spattering, unable, despite a series of expensive repairs, to find the silken mean its predecessor had so effortlessly achieved. Alas, it was not the reincarnation of my former love; it was a contemptible doppelgänger. Of course, I continued to write, but ever after, the feat of conjuring the first word, the first sentence, the first paragraph, has seemed more like work and less like magic.

When my friend Adam was sixteen, he bought, for twenty dollars, the letter book in which an eighteenth-century

Virginia merchant had copied his correspondence: reports on the price of tobacco, orders for molasses from the West Indies, letters to loyalist friends who had fled to Nova Scotia during the Revolutionary War. Stuck between the pages were hard yellowish scraps that Adam at first took to be fingernail parings. Then he noticed that one of the scraps had the barbs of a feather attached, and he realized that they were trimmings from a quill pen: fragments of a goose that had died during the reign of George III.

How inconvenient, but how glorious, it must have been to write with a feather (preferably the second or third follicle from a bird's left wing, which curved away from a right-handed writer). An eighteenth-century inkstand—complete with quill holder, penknife, inkwell, pounce box (to hold the desiccant powder), and wafer box (to hold the paste sealing wafers)—was a monument to the physical act of writing. But if no inkstand was at hand, one could make do with temporary expedients. One day, when Sir Walter Scott was out hunting, a sentence he had been trying to compose all morning suddenly leapt into his head. Before it could fade, he shot a crow, plucked a feather, sharpened the tip, dipped it in crow's blood, and captured the sentence.

For those who consider writing a form of romance, a Parker 51 can't hold a candle to a crow's feather, but it sure beats a cartridge pen, a ballpoint, a felt-tip, or a rollerball, especially those disposable models that proclaim, "Don't get too attached, I'm only a one-night stand." Pencils are fine in their way, but I prefer the immutability of ink. I still possess not only the poems I wrote at age ten but all the cross-outs: an even more telling index to my forgotten thought patterns. Richard Selzer, the surgeon and essayist, fills his fountain pen from a lacquered Chinese inkwell with a bronze dragon on its lid. To feed the genie that he says dwells therein, he mixes, from an old recipe, his own version of Higgins Eternal Ink, the brand he used when he learned to write sixty years ago. Eternal! To what other medium could that word possibly be applied?

A typewriter ribbon—if it's not self-correcting and if you don't use Wite-Out—may be permanent, but I would hardly call it eternal. The ichor of eternity belongs to India ink and crow's blood, not to machines. I admit the possibility, however, that typewriters, especially ancient manuals, can inspire in their owners the kind of fierce monogamy my pen inspired in me. When I worked at *Life* magazine, a veteran writer named Paul O'Neil was occasionally brought in to write crime stories. Once I saw Paul standing at the end of one of *Life*'s long corridors, rolling something down the carpet. It turned out he was wedded to a typewriter so old that its ribbons were no longer available, so whenever one gave out, he held one end of the worn-out ribbon, unspooled it with a bowler's underhand pitch, and then painstakingly rewound a fresh ribbon, cannibalized from another typewriter, onto the original spool. My mother feels the same kind of devotion to her Underwood, a venerable concatenation of levers, bars, gears, shafts, and a tiny silver bell whose ding, tolling the end of each line of type, hovers in the background of many of my childhood memories. My mother is eighty. Her father owned the typewriter before she was born. It was cleaned and repaired once, forty years ago. In 1989, when my parents moved, it languished in storage for several months while my mother made do with a portable Hermes. I asked her how she felt when she retrieved the Underwood. "It was like being reunited with a long-lost love," she said, "a love you've been married to all your life, but until you were parted you never realized how passionate you felt about him."

These days I use a computer. I am using it to write this essay, even though I should really be using a hand-whittled crow's feather. It is, as many writers have noted, unparalleled for revision. The Delete key is a boon to any writer who hates a cluttered page, although it makes the word processor the least eternal of all writing instruments. Cross-outs are usually consigned to oblivion. (I prefer to move the rejected phrases to the bottom of the screen, where they are continuously pushed ahead of the text-in-progress like an ever-burgeoning mound of snow before a plow.)

I am surprised by how much I like my computer, but I will never love it. I have used several; they seem indistinguishable. When you've seen one pixel you've seen them all. As a reader, I often feel I can detect the spoor of word processing in books, particularly long ones. The writers—no longer slowed by having to change their typewriter ribbons, fill their fountain pens, or sharpen their quills—tend to be prolix. I am especially suspicious of word-processed letters, which smell of boilerplate. Word-processed addresses are even worse. What a pleasure it is to open one's mailbox and find a letter from an old friend whose handwriting on the envelope is as instantly recognizable as a face!

I recently finished writing a book. I wrote its first sentence with a pen on August 7, 1991. (I remember the date because it was my birthday.) The intervening years—during which, not coincidentally, my handwriting became virtually illegible—marked my transition from pen to word processor. I had planned to write the last page of the book in longhand, partly for the sake of sentiment, partly because I thought a pen might decelerate my prose and make me especially careful where it counted most. But when the morning finally arrived after a furious all-nighter, and I realized I was only an hour from the end, I could no more halt my pell-mell rush than a marathoner could be persuaded to sniff the roses that lined the last hundred yards of the racecourse. It was too late. My old pen may be buried somewhere in my desk, but my Daemon, who surely would never take up residence in a Compaq Deskpro 4/25 Model 120, has either fled the premises or is now—I've got my fingers crossed—living inside me.

On Quality
Peter Brook

Quality is a word much used and much devalued today—one could even say it has lost its quality—yet all our lives we live according to an intuitive sense of its meaning, and it guides most of our attitudes and decisions. It has become fashionable to mistrust "value judgments," yet we appreciate people, we respond to their presence, we sense their feelings, we admire their skills, we condemn their actions, whether in cooking, politics, art, or love, in terms of unwritten hierarchies of quality.

Nothing illustrates this better than the curious phenomenon called art, which transforms the very nature of our perceptions and opens in us a sense of wonder, even of awe. Certain frequencies of vibrations—colors, shapes, geometric figures, and above all proportions—evoke corresponding frequencies in us, each of which has a specific quality or flavor. There is, for instance, a proportion within the rectangle called the Golden Section that will invariably produce a sensation of harmony, and here as in many other geometrical figures the psychological experience is inseparable from its mathematical description. Architecture has always observed and followed this marriage between feeling and proportion, and on a more intuitive level the painter and the sculptor are tirelessly correcting and refining their work so that its coarse outer crust can give way to the true inner feeling. A poet sifts within his thought pattern, giving attention to subtle intimations of sound and rhythm which are somewhere far behind the tumble of words with which his mind is filled. In this way, he creates a phrase that carries with it a new force, and the reader, in turn, can perceive his own feelings being intensified as their energy is transformed by the impressions he receives from the poem. In each case the difference is one of quality and is the result not of accident but of a unique process.

Excerpted from Peter Brook, "The Secret Dimension," in *Gurdjieff: Essays and Reflections on the Man and His Teachings*, ed. Jacob Needleman and George Baker (New York: The Continuum International Publishing Group Inc., 2004), pp. 31–32. First published in 1992.

The Eternal Secret
Stefan Zweig

After dinner we went over into the studio. It was a huge room, which contained replicas of most of [Rodin's] works, but amongst them lay hundreds of precious small studies—a hand, an arm, a horse's mane, a woman's ear, mostly only clay models. Today I can still recall exactly some of these sketches, which were made for his own practice, and could talk about them for an hour. Finally the master led me to a pedestal on which, covered with wet cloths, his latest work, a portrait of a woman, was hidden. With his heavy, furrowed peasant's hand he removed the cloths and stepped back. "Admirable," escaped from my lips, and at once I was ashamed of my banality. But with quiet objectivity in which not a trace of pride could have been found, he murmured, looking at his own work, merely agreeing: "*N'est-ce pas?*" Then he hesitated. "Only there at the shoulder … just a moment." He threw off his coat, put on a white smock, picked up a spatula, and with a masterly stroke on the shoulder smoothed the soft material so that it seemed the skin of a living, breathing woman. Again he stepped back. "And now here," he muttered. Again the effect was increased by a tiny detail. Then he no longer spoke. He would step forward, then retreat, look at the figure in a mirror, mutter and utter unintelligible sounds, make changes and corrections. His eyes, which at table had been amiably inattentive, now flashed with strange lights, and he seemed to have grown larger and younger. He worked, worked, worked, with the entire passion and force of his heavy body; whenever he stepped forward or back the floor creaked. But he heard nothing. He did not notice that behind him stood a young man, silent, with his heart in his throat, overjoyed that he was being permitted to watch this unique master at work. He had forgotten me entirely. I did not exist for him. Only the figure, the work, concerned him, and behind it, invisible, the vision of absolute perfection.

So it went on for a quarter or a half hour, I cannot recall how long. Great moments are always outside of time. Rodin was so engrossed, so rapt in his work that not even a thunder-stroke would have roused him. His movements became harder, almost angry. A sort of wildness or drunkenness had come over him; he worked faster and faster. Then his hands became hesitant. They seemed to have realized that there was nothing more for them to do. Once, twice, three times he stepped back without making any changes. Then he muttered something softly into his beard and placed the cloths gently about the figure as one places a shawl around the shoulders of a beloved woman. He took a deep breath and relaxed. His figure seemed to grow heavier again. The fire had died out. And then the incomprehensible occurred, the great lesson: he took off his smock, again put on his house-coat and turned to go. He had forgotten me completely in that hour of extreme concentration. He no longer knew that a young man whom he himself had led into the studio to show him his work had stood behind him with bated breath, as immovable as his statue.

He stepped to the door. As he started to unlock it, he discovered me and stared at me almost angrily: who was this young stranger who had slunk into his studio? But in the next moment he remembered and, almost ashamed, came towards me. "Pardon, Monsieur," he began. But I did not let him finish. I merely grasped his hand in gratitude. I would have preferred to kiss it. In that hour I had seen the eternal secret of all great art, yes, of every mortal achievement, made manifest: concentration, the collection of all forces, all senses, that *ecstasis*, that being-out-of-the-world of every artist. I had learned something for my entire lifetime.

Excerpted from Stefan Zweig, *The World of Yesterday: Memoirs of a European*, trans. Helmut Ripperger and B.W. Huebsch (Lincoln, Nebraska: University of Nebraska Press, 1964), pp. 147–149. First published in German as *Die Welt von Gestern* in 1942.

Must I Create?
Rainer Maria Rilke

There is only one thing you should do. Go into yourself. Find out the reason that commands you to write; see whether it has spread its roots into the very depths of your heart; confess to yourself whether you would have to die if you were forbidden to write. This most of all: ask yourself in the most silent hour of your night: *must* I write? Dig into yourself for a deep answer. And if this answer rings out in assent, if you meet this solemn question with a strong, simple "I *must*," then build your life in accordance with this necessity; your whole life, even into its humblest and most indifferent hour, must become a sign and witness to this impulse. Then come close to Nature. Then, as if no one had ever tried before, try to say what you see and feel and love and lose. Don't write love poems; avoid those forms that are too facile and ordinary: they are the hardest to work with, and it takes a great, fully ripened power to create something individual where good, even glorious, traditions exist in abundance. So rescue yourself from these general themes and write about what your everyday life offers you; describe your sorrows and desires, the thoughts that pass through your mind and your belief in some kind of beauty—describe all these with heartfelt, silent, humble sincerity, and, when you express yourself, use the things around you, the images from your dreams, and the objects that you remember. If your everyday life seems poor, don't blame *it*;

blame yourself; admit to yourself that you are not enough of a poet to call forth its riches; because for the creator there is no poverty and no poor, indifferent place. And even if you found yourself in some prison, whose walls let in none of the world's sounds—wouldn't you still have your childhood, that jewel beyond all price, that treasure house of memories? Turn your attention to it. Try to raise up the sunken feelings of this enormous past; your personality will grow stronger, your solitude will expand and become a place where you can live in the twilight, where the noise of other people passes by, far in the distance.

And if out of this turning-within, out of this immersion in your own world, *poems* come, then you will not think of asking anyone whether they are good or not. Nor will you try to interest magazines in these works: for you will see them as your dear natural possession, a piece of your life, a voice from it. A work of art is good if it has arisen out of necessity. That is the only way one can judge it. So, dear Sir, I can't give you any advice but this: to go into yourself and see how deep the place is from which your life flows; at its source you will find the answer to the question of whether you *must* create. Accept that answer, just as it is given to you, without trying to interpret it. Perhaps you will discover that you are called to be an artist. Then take that destiny upon yourself, and bear it, its burden and its greatness, without ever asking what reward might come from outside. For the creator must be a world for himself and must find everything in himself and in Nature, to whom his whole life is devoted.

But after this descent into yourself and into your solitude, perhaps you will have to renounce becoming a poet (if, as I have said, one feels one could live without writing, then one shouldn't write at all). Nevertheless, even then, this self-searching that I ask of you will not have been for nothing. Your life will still find its own paths from there, and that they may be good, rich, and wide, is what I wish for you, more than I can say.

Excerpted from Rainer Maria Rilke, *Letters to a Young Poet*, trans. Stephen Mitchell (New York: Modern Library, 2001), pp. 67–68. First published in German as *Briefe an einen jungen Dichter* in 1929.

The Forging
Jorge Luis Borges

Like the blind man whose hands are precursors
that push aside walls and glimpse heavens
slowly, flustered, I feel
in the crack of night
the verses that are to come.
I must burn the abominable darkness
in their limpid bonfire:
the purple of words
on the flagellated shoulder of time.
I must enclose the tears of evening
in the hard diamond of the poem.
No matter if the soul
walks naked and lonely as the wind
if the universe of a glorious kiss
still embraces my life.
The night is good fertile ground
for a sower of verses.

Translated from Spanish by Christopher Maurer.

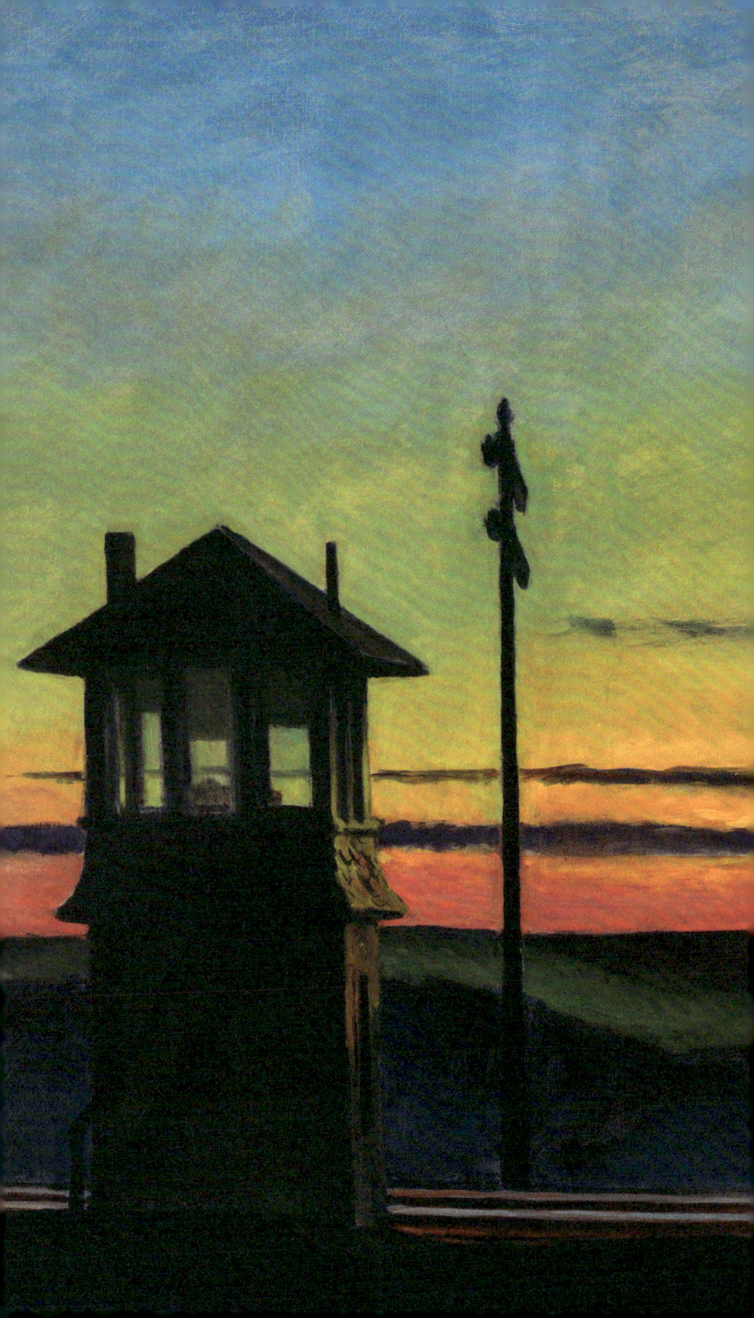

Interview with Wim Wenders
Jonathan Simons

While there remain many artists today whose careers stretch back to the fading era of analog filmmaking, few had the foresight to predict how much the mass proliferation of images would change the fabric of our society.

Born on the last day of the Second World War, Wim Wenders came of age during an era when cinema must have felt like stepping into a grainy dreamland, far removed from today's ultrabright and hyperreal digital storytelling. The phantasmagoric black-and-white films of Wenders' earliest years did not pretend to be reality. Enchantment was sweet but short-lived. Decades before the advent of digital video, celluloid was an expensive and vulnerable medium. An organic material subject to light, oxidization, and decay, its limitations prevented what mass media has now become, a glut of images colonizing our cities, our homes, and our minds.

Cinema was spectacle in its proper place, flickering fiction and wonderment as respite from lives otherwise firmly grounded in raw unmediated experience—real people doing real things in real places. A film maintained its singularity, its authority, its space; a film could take its time. And, unlike television, cinema centered on the largely solitary, contemplative act of sitting quietly on a chair for a few hours without interruption.

As early as the 1970s, Wim Wenders' work questioned how the commercialization of the image and the emergent domination of television culture threatened what he had come to love about cinema. In the opening scene of the 1974 film *Alice in the Cities*,[1] the first part of Wenders' *Road Movie* trilogy,[2] we find the fictional German reporter Phillip Winter hiding out under a boardwalk on Rockaway Beach in Queens, pensively examining his Polaroid study of the American landscape and singing "Under the Boardwalk" by The Drifters. Later, Winter destroys a television set in his motel room after John Ford's *Young Mr. Lincoln*[3] is brusquely interrupted by a commercial break. "I got completely lost," Winter says later. "It was a horrible journey. Once you leave New York City, nothing changes … the motels … the barbarous television." His companion replies: "That happens when you lose all sense of yourself."

Like the modernist masterpiece *The Waste Land* a half-century earlier, in which T.S. Eliot portrays the increasing fragmentation of postwar experience as a "heap of broken images," Winter spends the film taking his Polaroids,

---

[1] *Alice in the Cities*, directed by Wim Wenders (Munich: Filmverlag der Autoren, 1974), 16 mm, 112 minutes. Filmed in the United States, Germany, and the Netherlands.

[2] *Alice in the Cities* (1974), *The Wrong Move* (1975), and *Kings of the Road* (1976).

[3] *Young Mr. Lincoln*, directed by John Ford (Los Angeles: Twentieth Century Fox, 1939), 35 mm, 100 minutes. Filmed in California.

INTERVIEW WITH WIM WENDERS

struggling to figure out how they fit together—and how he fits into the commercial wasteland America has become. In Wenders' 1991 dystopian epic *Until the End of the World*,[4] perhaps his most prophetic film of all, the character Eugene asks, "In the beginning was the word. What would happen if only the image remained in the end?"

Wim Wenders is now a contemporary artist living in the dystopian moment he predicted decades ago. He has witnessed a cascade of technological changes in filmmaking, each propelled by this strange thirst we humans have for surrogate reality. But despite all the ways the digital revolution has triumphed, the thread of inquiry running through Wenders' fifty-plus years of work remains vital and unbroken—how does the artist rescue the fugitive fragments of stories and places from those heaps of broken images? And can they be put together in a way that wakes us up and reminds us how to see? "Why waste your life on disposable junk images?" Phillip says in *Lisbon Story*.[5] "Turn around and trust your eyes again."

JONATHAN SIMONS: You have books in so many of your films. In *Alice in the Cities*, there's the F. Scott Fitzgerald novel

---

[4] *Until the End of the World*, directed by Wim Wenders (Burbank, CA: Warner Bros, 1991), 35 mm, 158 and 287 minutes. Filmed in Germany, France, and Australia.

[5] *Lisbon Story*, directed by Wim Wenders (London: Axion Films, 1997), 35 mm, 103 minutes. Filmed in Portugal, Germany, and France.

Tender is the Night. Pessoa's *Always Astonished* is in *Lisbon Story*. Flaubert's *Sentimental Education* in *Wrong Move*. *Wings of Desire* features the Staatsbibliothek, the Berlin State Library. And Walt Whitman is hiding out in *Until the End of the World*. I feel as though you conceal books, like secret code, in your films. They must be extremely important for you.

WIM WENDERS: They are. I know the effort that goes into a book. And I like to hold a book in my hands. I can't read them all, unfortunately. Often, I buy a book simply because I like the way it looks, or because of its title. You can't judge a book by the cover, goes the famous blues song. But I do. And I love to write, although only in short formats: stories, reviews, essays, haikus. Actually, I write a lot, and I enjoy it very much. Everything else takes too long. Making a movie takes longer and longer nowadays. Anybody who says digital technology makes everything easier doesn't know what they're talking about. A lot of things take twice as long. It's easier to shoot, sure, but you end up with ten times as much material. And the editing is endless, because you don't shoot with the edit in mind anymore.

Peter Przygodda,[6] who was my editor for thirty-five years, was able to edit *American Friend* in three months! On film, on a good old analog editing table. We were still shooting

---

6 Peter Przygodda (1941–2011) was a German filmmaker and film editor.

in December and January, and by April we sent the print to Cannes. That would be totally unthinkable today.

JANOS TEDESCHI: Isn't it also because nowadays there is so much that can be done with the image in post-production?

WW: Yes. Before, there were very few transitions—dissolve, for instance, or fade to black. Now we have all sorts of different options, not to mention everything you can do with each individual image. I've watched contemporary cinematographers work on color corrections, and they'll spend the entire day on one shot! In the end, the final image is far removed from the original. Digital cinema is a whole different craft: every shot is created only at the end of the process. When you shoot, you are just establishing the blueprint for the actual image. That finds its shape later, with a lot of people having their say along the way.

JS: So do you try to push back against this or impose your own limitations?

WW: I do follow my own rules. I still try to envision the whole film beforehand. And knowing the freedom I'll have afterwards in the edit, I can enjoy a little more freedom as I shoot. Sometimes that's great. In *Wings of Desire*,[7] though, there was not a single special effect; it was all done in-camera. Today, of course, I include digital effects, or I know during the shoot what I'll need to add in post-production. Simplicity has become the most complex thing. Once, in film, there was simplicity, but that concept is lost now.

JT: In a 1988 essay, you wrote, "I'd like to raise concerns about the new medium's relationship to reality. That too could well turn out to be a moral issue. We all know how much the era of the digital storage of information has affected the notions of origin and reality."[8]

JS: We've been impressed by how much you predicted of what's going on now.

WW: It was already in the air, I guess. I remember working on my first commercials made with the help of digital technology—technology that hadn't really entered filmmaking yet. It was in those commercials that I had a first glimpse of the future. But it's true, it became a moral question.

---

7 *Wings of Desire*, directed by Wim Wenders (West Germany: Basis-Film-Verleih, 1987), 35 mm, 128 minutes. Filmed in West Germany and France.

8 Wim Wenders, *The Act of Seeing: Essays and Conversations*, trans. Michael Hofmann (London: Faber, 1997), p. 74.

JT: You went on to say, "And it's my dream that digital high-definition video could help sharpen our sense of reality. My nightmare, however, is that in the long run, it will only continue to undermine any remaining faith we may have in the truth of the image."[9]

WW: I'm one of the few filmmakers who has worked across that entire spectrum. I've worked with great technicians who began their careers in the silent era, like Henri Alekan, and with actors who previously starred in silent films by Fritz Lang. I actually did the first ever shoot in digital high definition, before anybody even knew it existed. And now I'm making films in digital 3D. I'm very happy that I was able to get to know that entire territory from its beginning. I've worked with people who were born with film and knew nothing else. And now I work with people who know nothing other than digital tools, young editors who will automatically go straight to the last take and start editing without watching all the previous takes, because they assume that if you shot it ten times, then the tenth take must be the best. Sometimes they're right. And sometimes the best take is the first one. But you need patience to find that out. And patience is not exactly the middle name of the digital age.

---

9 Ibid.

JT: I'm a filmmaker in my mid-thirties, and I've always shot digitally. But I enjoy analog photography. I develop my photographs at the end of the year to allow space between taking them and seeing them. I don't want the image to superimpose itself immediately on the reality that I see. It's so easy to take a picture nowadays. It's so easy to make a film. So what does the single image mean? And can we still see it?

WW: I'm in the middle of that question, and I have no answer. I recently took my first ever journey with a digital camera. I traveled through China for four weeks, and I took thousands and thousands of pictures. Normally I would have returned with a few hundred. I turned off the damn screen on the back of the camera because I didn't want to keep looking at it, so I only used the viewfinder. That was last year, but I'm still afraid to look at that abundance of pictures. It's simply overwhelming. I tried once; there were just too many of them, and I gave up.

JS: Actually, there are algorithms which could search through your trove of photos and pick out the ones you might like.

WW: And probably some of them would be right on the money. I still buy a lot of CDs and LPs, every now and then on the Internet. The algorithm will immediately suggest I listen to this or that as well, and I feel inclined to do so, because maybe it knows something I don't. And all of a sudden you realize your musical taste has been taken away from you.

JT: And the same for books.

WW: Movies too, probably.

JT: And movies too. There's just so much now. Netflix overwhelms you with all the things you should see. I read an article recently about how Hollywood is starting to use machine-learning to write scripts. You put in a few keywords, and the algorithm writes the script based on all the other scripts of movies that have been successful in the marketplace.

WW: It's the same for scores. Some scores already sound as if an algorithm has written them.

JS: In the 1990s, you created a five-hour-long film, *Until the End of the World*. Can you imagine anyone going into a theater now to watch a film of that length? When a new film is released, it's in theaters for a very short period of time, if at all, and then it goes straight to streaming. Cinemas are shuttering, and the future of film seems bleak to me. What do you think?

ww: Well, on the other hand, many people spend hours every night watching series. And at least in a series, there's a huge spectrum of characters that are far more developed than they usually are in a movie.

js: With Netflix and other streaming services now at the center of so many people's lives, has television won?

ww: Television, at its core, was programmed, which meant that you had to stick to a certain viewing schedule. But that is gone now. You can watch all day long and sleep at night. Or you can watch all night and sleep all day. Television never imagined itself like that. What we have now is not really "television" anymore. It's a strange new thing.

jt: Maybe the question nowadays is not so much whether television or series are taking over, but whether going to a movie theater and really opening yourself up to the experience is gone.

js: You seem like the rare individual who has straddled both sides of the digital revolution. You're critical of new digital tools, yet you are also experimental and open to working with them. I'm wondering how that tension plays out for you.

ww: I haven't come to peace with it. It's still a struggle. Sticking to your guns gets difficult. Everything is planned out and streamlined. I've decided to make more documentaries, because at least nobody expects you to know at the start of the project how the film is going to end. Maybe the high demand for documentaries at the moment reflects that freedom. They are a beautifully open territory that the algorithms haven't really accessed yet.

js: The question you seem to have been asking yourself all these years is how to continue to make films when the world is flooded with images.

ww: Filmmaking as a language still has a lot of freedom, and, like any language, it tries to make sense of the world. The only justification for producing more work is that I feel a certain necessity in doing so, in continuing to make sense of a world that is experiencing radical change.

js: The one thing that seems consistent throughout all your films—both fiction and documentaries—is that we often see characters simply sitting around thinking. And you are certainly not afraid of long takes. Do you feel that there is still an audience who takes the time to fully appreciate and contemplate your films?

ww: Well, there are still people who *do* think, who *do* contemplate, who *do* read, people who sing, pray, create, or do things on their own, but you also realize that most people you meet are driven by something external, something they receive, and that is definitely a development we are unable to go back on now. You start wondering about children and why kids don't watch movies anymore, the way we used to, and why they become addicted to stuff so quickly.

For me, the process of reading was essential to becoming who I am. I actually learned to read before I went to school out of sheer necessity because my grandmother couldn't read very well herself. I followed her finger and learned by intuition. I learned to recognize words and then started to read a book a day for years. I read all night long and invested all my money in batteries so I could read at night. Eventually I discovered that my chemistry set had this little phosphorescent plate which, when you shone light on it, enabled you to read for a minute. I could save big time on batteries! Much later, I got worried, thinking about all the nights of my life reading by phosphorescent light, when I learned that it was radioactive, or somehow harmful—they don't even use it on watch dials anymore. And yet I read all of Karl May in this way. Once a minute, I quickly flashed light on the phosphorescent plate, and then it was fully active for another minute. I read and read and read.

Now I see my niece, and all she wants to do is read. I'm so happy that there is a kid who doesn't want to watch television in the evening like her little brother. She just wants books. And when you ask her, "What do you want?" she says she wants books. And I'm so happy, because I know this girl is going to be well equipped for an independent life.

JT: I'm interested in something you said about *Until the End of the World*: "The essential idea was actually the realization that, globally speaking, our entire civilization had transitioned, or was transitioning, from a culture of the word to a culture of the image."

WW: That's what I truly believed when I was making the film: I was making a movie about the future of our visual culture. At the end of the shoot, together with my "digital advisor" (there wasn't even a name yet for his job), I went to Tokyo to work on the dream sequences. We had been granted access by NHK[10] to their prototype editing suite. It was entirely digital and HD. Nobody else had used it before. We realized that if we fed footage into the equipment and played it on fast forward, it would pixelate. We were the first people on the planet to see the effect of that pixelization, and we decided that we needed to record it: we had found a kind of

---

10 Japan Broadcasting Corporation.

language we could use for our dreams. Something that was different from film language.

In order to make a film about my theory, we had to become victims of it. We stayed in that editing suite, not for the three weeks that we had initially booked, but for three months. We lived in it. We slept in it. We were completely addicted. We had huge shadows under our eyes. When we staggered outside in the middle of the night for a drink or something, we were zombies suffering from the same disease the film was about.

JS: You basically gave people a picture of screen addiction twenty years before the iPhone came out. In the past, you've talked about the increasing ubiquity of images in much starker terms than you do now. You don't seem as outraged as you used to be.

WW: No, I don't feel outraged, because I've accepted that this is the future. Tarantino still shoots on film, and as far as I know, Spielberg even edits on Moviolas, but maybe that's a rumor. In any case, they're definitely the dinosaurs. Everybody else works with and watches their stuff on digital machines. Nobody watches projected movies anymore.

The other day, Ang Lee, a huge 3D aficionado, showed me his last film, shot at a hundred and twenty frames per second in 3D.[11] Everything was so fluid, and even when people were in motion, every pore of the skin, every movement of the eyes and the mouth was there. On film, this has never been the case. We're used to people appearing blurry when they move quickly. What Ang showed me was a whole new ballgame. He is convinced that this is the future of movies—although the industry doesn't necessarily think so, because it's far more expensive.

JS: But do you really want to see that much information?

WW: That is a good question. I asked Ang Lee exactly that. I was very impressed with the film, but I asked him, "Do you think people really want to take in so much?"

JS: I think the more advanced these technologies are, the more they take us out of ourselves. With grainy film, like some of your earlier work, the lack of perfection pushes you back on yourself; you can't fully buy into the image.

WW: You start reading between the lines, like you do with a book, and you dream yourself into the story. But the viewer today isn't given that responsibility anymore, isn't given the

---

11 *Gemini Man*, directed by Ang Lee (Hollywood: Paramount, 2019), DCP-2K and HFR-4K, 117 minutes.

chance to add anything of his or her own. What you see is what you get.

JS: If I were in your shoes, I would feel a certain freedom knowing that I had reached a point where I didn't have to bow to the norms or expectations of today's cinema. I could just do my own thing. Do you feel that way at all?

WW: I do, somehow. And I feel it's a privilege. I feel I am old enough to insist on doing something that I stand for, and which might therefore be "unwatchable" for some people. You know, recently, for the first time in my life, I made a 3D film that is on restricted release. It will never be seen in theaters, will never be distributed. You have to go to a museum for it. Right now it can be seen at the Fondation Beyeler.[12]

JT: How does that make you feel?

WW: It is a strange return to a painterly state. There is still an incredible difference between standing in front of a painting and seeing it reproduced. You're involved, and you're implicated, and all of your senses are intact. It's a very complex

---

12 A modern and contemporary art museum near Basel, Switzerland. As part of its Spring 2020 exhibition *Edward Hopper*, Fondation Beyeler screened Wim Wenders' 3D film installation *Two or Three Things I Know about Edward Hopper*.

experience. You stand there, and you're mesmerized, and you are grateful that you have the privilege to be there.

In this museum, you turn from Edward Hopper paintings and go into a movie theater, and you see fifteen minutes of film which you can only see right there, the way you just saw the paintings. It reminds me of when I first saw *The Rules of the Game*,[13] the Renoir film. I went to the earliest screening, ten o'clock in the morning, at a theater in Paris. And I stayed there until midnight. I watched the film six, seven times in a row. Sometimes I was the only one in the theater. And I felt very privileged. I felt I had seen the original because I had spent all day in that place with it. When I finally came out, I knew I would probably not see the film again for years.

JS: I want to ask you a couple of questions that I hope will sound very familiar to you: the questions you said you ask whenever you're interviewing others. Where does your work begin? And what's the first step you take?

WW: First, I see a place. And its specific light. For instance: you come out of a movie theater in northern Finland and it's the middle of the night, way after midnight, but the sun is lingering over the horizon the most beautiful sunset. And there's

---

13 *The Rules of the Game*, directed by Jean Renoir (Neuilly-sur-Seine, France: Gaumont, 1939), 35 mm, 110 minutes.

no need to go to bed, because the sun is still there, so you walk, and you meet people. And then you arrive at a square, and they're playing tango music. Everybody's dancing. It's the Midnight Sun Film Festival, and by now it's two o'clock in the morning, and there are a hundred people dancing tango. It's not complicated, it's not artistry—it's a sort of shuffling around. Then you realize that it's the national dance and everybody's pretty drunk. But it's peaceful, and the sun just hangs there. There's such clarity of light.

All my best films begin with places. Sometimes for me, the first step in making a film is arriving in a place I don't know, liking it very much, and feeling that it is charged with stories that are worth pursuing.

This conversation between Analog Sea founder Jonathan Simons, Analog Sea editor Janos Tedeschi, and Wim Wenders took place on January 21, 2020 in a small cottage in the west of Switzerland.

Alice in the Cities
Wim Wenders

What's so barbaric about this TV is not that it chops up everything and interrupts it with ads, although that's already bad enough; far worse is that everything it shows also turns into advertising, into ads for the status quo. All those TV images come down to the same common ugly message, a kind of vicious contempt. No images leave you in peace: they all want something from you.

Excerpt transcribed from *Alice in the Cities*, directed by Wim Wenders (Munich: Filmverlag der Autoren, 1974), 16 mm, 112 minutes. Filmed in the United States, Germany, and the Netherlands.

Smashing the Television
Alexander Graf

The American setting for the first half of *Alice in the Cities* is highly relevant. Hollywood has been the strongest influence on Wenders' filmmaking, evidenced in his adaptation of essentially American genres such as the road movie in *Alice*; film noir in *The State of Things, The Goalie's Anxiety at the Penalty Kick, The American Friend,* and the Western genre in *Kings of the Road* and *Paris, Texas*. But *Alice in the Cities* is also the film in which Wenders begins to relativize his idealistic picture of America as "the land of free vision."[1] Beginning to question the validity of the "American Dream," exported to all parts of the world through American musical and cinematic culture, Wenders here uses his film to announce the death of the mythical American cinema of the 1940s and 1950s that had so inspired him, finding one reason for its extinction in the kind of vision and visuality nurtured by the television phenomenon and the commercial interests it represents. The television set that the protagonist Philip Winter later destroys in his hotel room is showing a film by John Ford, *Young Mr. Lincoln*,[2] when the film is interrupted by advertising. That is the point at which Winter gets up from his bed and knocks the

---

[1] Peter W. Jansen and Wolfram Schütte, *Wim Wenders* (Munich: Carl Hanser, 1992), p. 148.

[2] *Young Mr. Lincoln*, directed by John Ford (Los Angeles: Twentieth Century Fox, 1939), 35 mm, 100 minutes. Filmed in California.

television set from its table, suggesting that television, rather than the film itself, provokes the unusually aggressive outburst in the normally composed Winter.

The last sequence of *Alice in the Cities* completes the picture when we see the headline announcing Ford's death in a newspaper Winter is reading. The associations made in the introductory sequence, the final sequence, and in the motel sequence when Winter smashes the television set are complex but fully consistent with Wenders' belief that it is above all the introduction of television and the resulting inflation of commercialized images that brought about the demise of the mythical American cinema that was such an inspiration to him and many other filmmakers of his generation.

In his 1970 article on Ford, "Emotion Pictures: Slowly Rockin' On," Wenders describes what he misses about Ford's cinema: "I miss the friendliness, the care, the thoroughness, the seriousness, the peace, the humanity of John Ford's films; I miss those faces that are never forced into anything; those landscapes that aren't just backgrounds."[3]

Wenders' character Winter would like to believe in the promised dream but finds that it is empty in a land where images have pervaded every aspect of life, to the extent that he, in a sense, becomes blinded by them. With the announcement

---

3 Wim Wenders, *Emotion Pictures: Reflections on the Cinema*, trans. Sean Whiteside (London: Faber and Faber, 1991), pp. 49–50.

of Ford's death at the end of the film, the camera rises from the train that is taking Alice and Winter to Munich until it is high enough for a panoramic shot of the whole surrounding landscape up to the horizon that fills the frame. Wenders sought to give the impression of seeing all Germany in this shot and wanted to fly as high as possible.[4] After the forests of signposts, urban and suburban streets and the psychological numbness of the American city and landscape, Germany—Europe—appears like a clean sheet of paper, an emptiness soothing to the eye, an as yet undiscovered land that offers the opportunity and the invitation to explore, discover, and perhaps find a new story. This last sequence exhibits the type of panoramic shot that Wenders praises in Ford's films, that he considers to be present only in contemporary American music. It is but a dream of America, a land where the visible has become so predominant that it leads to blindness.

---

4 Filippo D'Angelo, *Wim Wenders* (Milan: Editrice Il Castoro, 1994), p. 9.

Adapted from Alexander Graf, *The Cinema of Wim Wenders: The Celluloid Highway* (New York: Wallflower Press, 2002), pp. 72–75.

The Old Master John Ford
Harry Tomicek

History told through *music*. History told through *images*, which often feel like archetypes or concentrated dreams—real, but also *hyper*-real; *everyday*, yet otherworldly. The essence, the *spirit* of something made into an image through contemplation, condensed into long takes. The sight of the women watching the soldiers leave, one of them whispering that she can barely make them out anymore; all she can see are the flags.[1] The sight of returnees wreathed in dust, while still anxious women scan the serried riders and stretchers for their living, wounded, or dead husbands.[2] Or the sight of the provincial lawyer and later sixteenth president riding tall and serene on an undersized mule towards his first courtroom appearance in Springfield, Illinois, like a Don Quixote in top hat and frock coat.[3]

These are sometimes dark, sometimes lushly comic tales of America—a real country, but also one sung, one cinematically dreamed into being by Ford; a country born of his visions. This is not the U.S. cavalry, but *Ford's* cavalry;

---

[1] *Fort Apache*, directed by John Ford (New York: RKO Radio Pictures, 1948), 35 mm, 125 minutes. Filmed in California, Utah, and Arizona.

[2] *Rio Grande*, directed by John Ford (Los Angeles: Republic Pictures, 1950), 35 mm, 105 minutes. Filmed in California, Utah, and Arizona.

[3] *Young Mr. Lincoln*, directed by John Ford (Los Angeles: Twentieth Century Fox, 1939), 35 mm, 100 minutes. Filmed in California.

these are not the pioneers, but *Ford's* pioneers; not Lincoln, but *Ford's* dream of the man. A dream of heartfelt conviction, but also a cool, funny, smart, terse, and witty one: a legend told in the pithy present tense.

Translated from German by Jozef van der Voort for Analog Sea.

The Lost World
Siegfried Schober

His death is no shock, but seems natural—almost incidental—for John Ford lived a long life (seventy-eight years) and did a great deal (over one hundred films). By the time he was so strangely rediscovered here in Germany, he was already part of the distant past—alive and present only in and as memory, much like the people and stories in his films.

Like something from long, long ago. That's how one's own enthusiasm for John Ford feels today, and it was in the same vein that Peter Handke wrote about him in his American novel, an attempt replete with enchantment and longing to recover a lost world, not so much for the sake of that world as for the salvation of his own humanity. "I'm going to tell him that I learned about America from that picture, that it taught me to understand history by seeing people in nature."[1]

These lines also refer to a romantic yearning for humane, poetic, yet immediate relationships such as we often find—or perhaps rather peer into—in Ford's films; the barbaric conditions and broken figures that fundamentally shape his pictures, ephemerally. "On the hilltop we sat in the grass and looked down into the valley. He lit a cigar with a big kitchen match. 'I always want to be with people,' said John Ford. 'When I'm

---

1 Peter Handke, *Short Letter, Long Farewell*, trans. Ralph Manheim (New York: Farrar, Straus and Giroux, 1974), p. 171.

with people, I always want to be the last to leave, because I don't want any of them to run me down when I'm gone. Besides, I want to be there to make sure nobody runs down anybody else who's left. That's been my principle in making my pictures.'"[2]

---

[2] Ibid., pp. 247–248.

Excerpted from Siegfried Schober, "Verlorene Welt," in *Süddeutsche Zeitung* (September 3, 1973), p. 14. Translated by Jozef van der Voort for Analog Sea. In Wim Wenders' 1974 film *Alice in the Cities,* Philip Winter (played by Rüdiger Vogler) is seen reading this article while seated on the train.

A Language of Images
Wim Wenders

All of a sudden, on the turbulent streets of Tokyo, I realized that a valid image of this city might very well be an electronic one, and not only my sacred, celluloid images. In its own language, the video camera was capturing this city in an appropriate way. I was shocked. A language of images was not the privilege of cinema. Wasn't it necessary then to re-evaluate everything, all notions of identity, language, images, authorship? Perhaps our future authors will be makers of commercials, or video clips, or the designers of electronic games and computer programs. And movies? This nineteenth-century invention, this art of the mechanical age, this beautiful language of light and movement, of myth and adventure, that can speak of love and hate, of war and peace, of life and death, what would become of it? And all these craftsmen behind the cameras, behind the lights, at the editing tables, would they have to unlearn everything? Would there ever be an electronic craftsman, a digital craftsman? And would this new electronic language be capable of showing the men of the twentieth century like the still camera of August Sander or the film camera of John Cassavetes?

Excerpt transcribed from *Notebooks on Cities and Clothes*, directed by Wim Wenders (Berlin: Road Movies Filmproduktion GmbH, 1988), 35 mm, 81 minutes. Filmed in Paris and Tokyo.

The Photographic Experience
Susan Sontag

Needing to have reality confirmed and experience enhanced by photographs is an aesthetic consumerism to which everyone is now addicted. Industrial societies turn their citizens into image-junkies; it is the most irresistible form of mental pollution. Poignant longings for beauty, for an end to probing below the surface, for a redemption and celebration of the body of the world—all these elements of erotic feeling are affirmed in the pleasure we take in photographs. But other, less liberating, feelings are expressed as well. It would not be wrong to speak of people having a *compulsion* to photograph: to turn experience itself into a way of seeing. Ultimately, having an experience becomes identical with taking a photograph of it, and participating in a public event comes more and more to be equivalent to looking at it in photographed form. That most logical of nineteenth-century aesthetes, Mallarmé, said that everything in the world exists in order to end in a book. Today everything exists to end in a photograph.

Excerpted from Susan Sontag, "In Plato's Cave," in *On Photography* (London: Penguin Classics, 2008), p. 24. First published in 1977.

Once
Jonathan Simons

Once,
in a garden in Rossinière,
in the shadow of Balthus's grave,
sipping Setsuko's heady tea
from fragile porcelain,
we shattered the silence
cracking chestnuts
with the bottoms
of heavy glasses.

Twenty-four times a second,
the hungry lens bites at reality,
and then beautiful replicas
illuminate the walls of our caves.

Once,
in a garden in Rossinière,
sipping tea with Wim,
infinity stretched out
its wild and capable body.

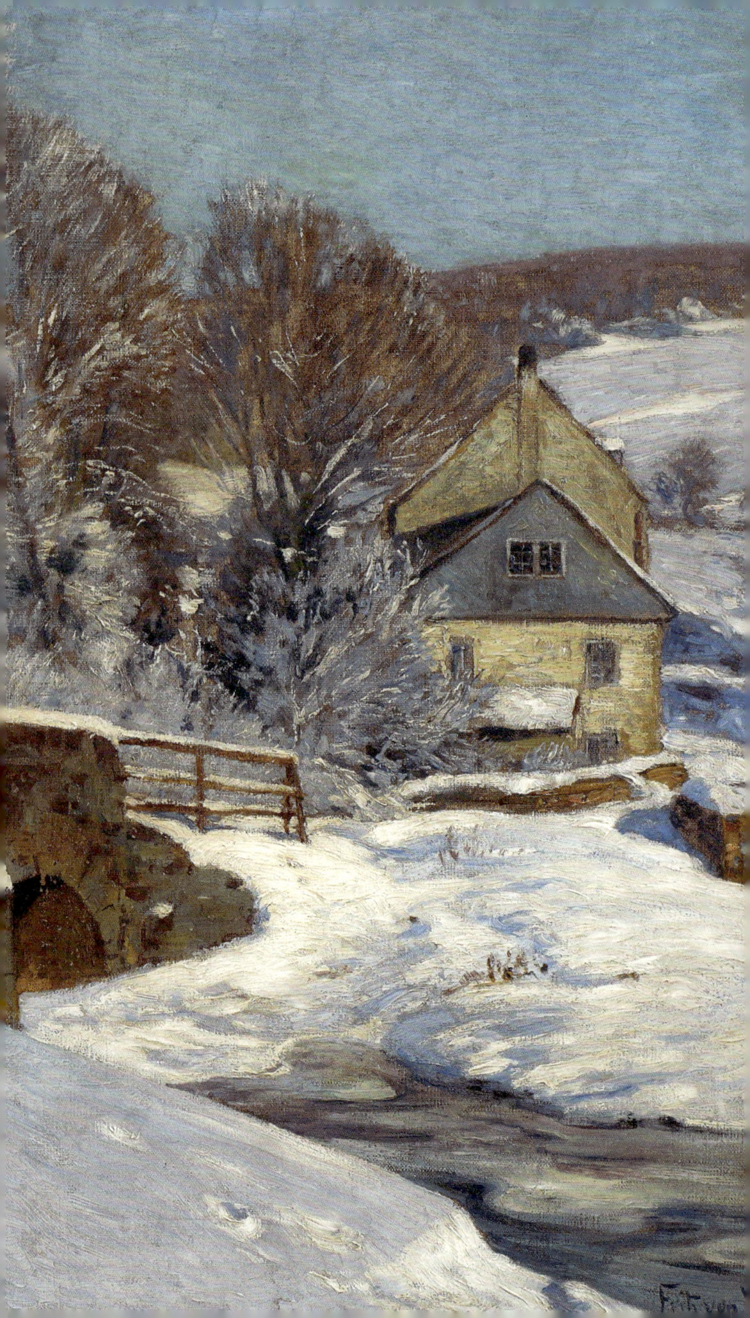

Adagissimo
Leonard Bernstein

One day in 1962, I received a call from Glenn Gould in Toronto. He was to play Brahms' D Minor Concerto with me and the New York Philharmonic the following week in Carnegie Hall. He said, "Oh boy, have I got some surprises for you; I have made such discoveries about this piece." I thought, "Well, wonderful." Any discovery of Glenn's was welcomed by me because I worshiped the way he played: I admired his intellectual approach, his "guts" approach, his complete dedication to whatever he was doing, his constant inquiry into a new angle or a new possibility of the truth of a score. That's why he made so many experimental changes of tempi. He would play the same Mozart sonata movement *adagio* one time and *presto* the next, when actually it's supposed to be neither. He was not trying to attract attention but looking for the truth. I loved that in him.

A week before he was to come to New York, he made that call to announce that he had some really new ideas about the Brahms, and to prepare me for them. I said, "Along what order? You're not making a big cut? You're not taking a huge repeat that Brahms didn't write?" Because he had made it sound so extraordinary, I didn't know what to expect. He said, "No, it's just a matter of tempo here and there, but I just want to warn you because you might be a little shocked."

I told him nothing he could do would shock me because I knew him too well by now, and I was almost unshockable.

He arrived and set forth three unbelievable tempi for the three movements. In the first place, they were so slow that the first movement alone took about as much time as it should take to play the whole concerto. It was all in six—the whole first movement had to be beaten in six. There was no sense of *alla breve*, which, of course, is the point of the movement—or, rather, there was no sense of that fine line between 6/4 in *two* and 6/4 in *six*. It's a kind of tightrope which you walk so that at any moment you can veer toward one side or the other—be more flowing, or be more *sostenuto*, whatever—according to the needs of the music. This, however, was no tightrope. This was having fallen off the tightrope into the safety net called *adagissimo*—and this for an *allegro*, mind you. I said I was perfectly willing to go along with it, *pour le sport*, so to speak, as maybe he had something there.

I also said that I thought we'd have an empty house before we got to the slow movement. Glenn laughed. "Wait till you hear how the slow movement goes, which is also in 6/4. It's exactly the same as the first movement's 6/4. It's just like *repeating!*" That was his major discovery: the two movements were really both aspects of the same movement, and therefore both had to be the same. […]

I did forewarn the orchestra a little about this. I said, "Now, don't give up, because this is a great man, whom we have to take very seriously." There were some very odd looks when we began the rehearsal, but they were wonderfully cooperative and went right along with it. Of course, they did get tired: it *was* very tiring. After the rehearsal I asked him, "Are you sure you're still convinced about the 'slowth' of this piece?" And he said, "Oh, more than ever; did you hear how wonderfully the tension built?"

In those days, we had our first concert of each weekly series on Thursday night, which was a kind of dress rehearsal in which I talked to the audience. It was a chic night, *the* night to be there. You could never get a ticket for Thursday night. I sometimes had a piano and illustrated points about the music being played as I do on a television show, all in order to bring the audience closer to the music. That night I thought, "What am I going to talk to them about?"—when obviously the main subject of the evening was going to be our performance of a Brahms concerto and Glenn's interpretation of it. So I said to Glenn backstage, "You know, I have to talk to the people. How would it be if I warned them that it was going to be very slow, and prepare them for it?" […] It wasn't to be a disclaimer; I was very much interested in the results—particularly the audience reaction to it. I wrote down a couple of notes on the back of an envelope and showed them to Glenn: "Is this okay?" And he said, "Oh, it's wonderful, what a great idea."

So I went out, read these few notes, and said, "This is gonna be different, folks. And it's going to be very special. This is the

Glenn Gould Brahms concerto." Out he came, and indeed he played it exactly the way he had rehearsed it, and wonderfully too. The great miracle was that nobody left, because of course it had become such a thing to listen to. The house came down, although, if I remember correctly, it took well over an hour to play. It was very exciting. I never loved him more.

The result in the papers, especially the *New York Times*, was that I had betrayed my colleague. Little did they know—though I believe I did say so to the audience—that I had done this with Glenn's encouragement. They just assumed that I had sold him down the river by coming out first to disclaim his interpretation. It was, on the contrary, a way of educating the audience as part of Thursday night's procedure. All this was not only misunderstood, but repeated and repeated and multiplied exponentially by every other newspaper that wrote about it. […]

Of course, a defense is very weak once a legend is born. […] I have the feeling, even now, that trying to make this story about Glenn clear by telling the truth can't really erase the now legendary, but false, version.

Glenn laughed about it. He has that kind—had that kind of … (I can't get used to this idea of putting him in the past tense)—Glenn had strong elements of sportsmanship and teasing, the kind of daring which accounts for his freshness, the great sense of inquiry which made him suddenly understand Schoenberg and Liszt in the same category, or Purcell

ADAGISSIMO

and Brahms, or Orlando Gibbons and Petula Clark. He would suddenly bring an unlikely pair of musicians together in some kind of startling comparative essay.

At some point, early on—I think when he was doing the Beethoven C Minor Concerto with me—Glenn and I were going to do some work at my apartment, so I invited him to dinner first. This was the first time Felicia, my wife, had actually met him. As you know, Glenn had a "cold complex." He had a fur hat on all the time, several pairs of gloves, and I don't know how many mufflers, and coat upon coat. He arrived and began taking off all, or at least some, of these things, and Felicia met and loved him instantly. "Oh," she said, "aren't you going to take off your hat?" He had a fur astrakhan cap on, and he said, "Well, I don't think so." At length, he did, and there was all this rotting, matted, sweaty hair that hadn't been shampooed in God knows how long. It was disappearing because it was so unhealthy. Before I knew it, Felicia—before "Have a drink" or anything—had him in the bathroom, washed his hair and cut it, and he emerged from the bathroom looking like an angel. I've never seen anything so beautiful as Glenn Gould coming out of that bathroom with his wonderful blond clean hair.

There was a marvelous relationship that sprang up instantly between Glenn and Felicia which lasted through the years. I remember when during the summer of 1955—several years before we met Glenn—Felicia was waiting to give birth to our son, Alexander. The doctors had miscalculated, so we had an extra month to wait. It was June; there was a heat wave in New York; she was in her ninth month and very easily tired and disgruntled. One of the great sources of comfort to us during that month was Glenn's first recording of the *Goldberg Variations* which had just come out. It became "our song."

Of course, the haircut Felicia gave Glenn didn't change his lifestyle at all. I remember we had a recording session a week after the dinner, and he had the fur cap and gloves back on along with all the rest of it. He'd whip the gloves off, record a few bars and then whip them on again, or he'd stop suddenly in the middle of a take and race downstairs to the men's room to warm his hands under hot water. He'd come back, gloves on, and start again. He was very unpredictable, but always very approachable. He had a strange combination of dogmaticism and great humor, which don't usually go together. The humor never, to my knowledge, went away.

The one time I saw him on his own turf, so to speak, was when I was making a Canadian tour with the New York Philharmonic, and we stopped in Toronto. Naturally I had to call up Glenn. I went to see him at his apartment, which was a shambles—months of mail stacked up along with newspapers and test pressings. You had to pick your way between piles of things. There he was in the midst of all this, at his special Chickering piano, which he had prepared to sound rather like a fortepiano, or as much like a harpsichord as possible.

ADAGISSIMO

I wanted to see his apartment and said, "Oh, this must be the bedroom," but he wouldn't let me go in—apparently it was an even worse mess. In any case, he said, "Let's go and do my favorite thing." So we went down and got into his car, he being wrapped up in all his furs and gloves and hats, with all the windows up, the heat turned on full blast, and the radio turned on to a good music station, also full blast. We drove around the city of Toronto, just listening to the radio and sweating. I couldn't stop sweating, but he loved it. I said, "Do you do this often?" He said, "Every day."

This was a man who was fascinated by the Arctic and the North Pole. In fact, at that very time he was making the incredible documentary about the North. He'd been there twice and was just about to go again because he was so fascinated by it. For this man, who was so afraid of the cold, to be attracted to the cold is a paradox that only twelve Freuds could figure out.

Here was a man you could really come to love. We became very close friends, but when he stopped playing in public, I saw less and less of him. I regret that, because it was a real relationship, based on a mutual appreciation of the sense of inquiry. He had an intellect that one could really play against and learn from. He was about fifteen years younger than I, I think, but I never felt that he was my junior. He was a real peer, in every sense. When he died, I just couldn't bear it.

The North as Archetype
Howard Fink

The *Idea of North*, the opening program in Glenn Gould's *Solitude Trilogy*, was broadcast on CBC radio in 1967.[1] It was the first of seven full-length programs in an experimental radio genre of Gould's own invention, which he called "contrapuntal documentary." As the term suggests, he combined musical composition with documentary in these programs, but, as he clearly explained, he also incorporated a form of radio drama practiced by the CBC. The documentary theme of *The Idea of North*—the idea, or experience, of "North-ness"—relates to the general theme of the *Solitude Trilogy*: human isolation in modern society, and the search for a reaffirmation of human and ethical values. Gould developed the syncretic genre of contrapuntal documentary as the most effective instrument for communicating this theme, and for combining his didactic and creative goals.

The average listener to *The Idea of North*, confronted by Gould's label "documentary," recognizes the theme of

---

1 *The Idea of North*, produced by Gould in monaural sound in the CBC studios, with the technical assistance of Lorne Tulk, was broadcast as a CBC special. According to Tulk, in a 1991 interview with me, the equipment for this production was relatively primitive, and much of the work consisted of cutting and splicing—almost by hand—many hundreds of separate elements. *North* was rebroadcast by the CBC in 1969, at which time Gould prepared and read an introduction that revealed his creative methods and purposes in this production, and defined its major themes.

THE NORTH AS ARCHETYPE

"North-ness" but looks in vain for the comfort of certain characteristic documentary techniques—for a logical advancing of the theme, for a continuity controlled by a principal editorial voice, and (especially for most of the second half) for any clear and uninterrupted voice amid the contrapuntal weaving of voices and sounds. *North* can be defended as, ultimately, a musical composition that makes use of voices and sounds in a way that is common in some twentieth-century music—music admired by Gould—and the identification of *North* as music does fit with the accepted view of Gould as a musician.

Unfortunately, the problem of defining its form is made even more complex by Gould's own acknowledgement that *North* was influenced by the radio drama of the CBC's Golden Age in the 1940s and 1950s. This relationship is reinforced and refined by Klaus Schöning, founder of the Studio for Acoustical Art of the German Radio Network, who acknowledges *North* as an influential early example of experimental radio drama—what Schöning calls the "*neue Hörspiel*" or "*ars acustica*." The form Gould developed for *North*, and which he applied to his other contrapuntal documentaries, is complex and syncretic, and to understand it one must suspend preconceptions about both the form and its creator.

Gould, as we know, was a pianist of genius who impressed concert audiences with his control and dexterity, and with the sensitivity, depth, and complexity of his interpretations, though he often experimented with the likes of piano preparation. We know about Gould's decision to forsake the concert stage in 1964, because he felt that playing up to a live audience necessarily distorted his relationship to the music. We know about his turning to the sound studio to edit his taped performances, capitalizing on the flexibility of the electronic media in order to help modulate his playing, so as to approach ever closer to his conception of the ideal musical performance.

We also know that Gould extended his creative range by composing a small number of conventional musical works, but more serious were the seven radio documentaries he created between 1967 and 1979. The first three, the *Solitude Trilogy*, were on more general and philosophical subjects: *The Idea of North*, on the Canadian Arctic; *The Latecomers* (1969), on Newfoundland; and *The Quiet in the Land* (1977), on the Mennonites of Manitoba. But what followed were four documentaries on musical figures: Stokowski (1971), Casals (1974), Schoenberg (1974), and Richard Strauss (1979). Gould also wrote music for several films, including those based on Kurt Vonnegut's novel *Slaughterhouse-Five* (1972) and Canadian Timothy Findley's novel *The Wars* (1982). And he hosted a large number of mainly musical series and special programs on CBC radio and television, producing many of these himself.

But emphasis on the musical cannot completely account for Gould's creative intentions and achievements, particularly with *The Idea of North* and the other contrapuntal documentaries he made, even though his own description of *North* does include musical terms. A complete explanation of the genre of *North* involves musical techniques but is also closely related to the forms of documentary and drama as practiced in Canadian radio of the Golden Age. Gould was, in fact, a child of the radio generation of the 1930s and 1940s, the decades before television. He confessed to Lorne Tulk, his technician on *North*, that he was an avid radio listener, especially to radio dramas of all kinds, from the most popular to the most serious. And he remarked that in *North* he applied the concepts of sound drama to documentary. A unified theory of *North* must account for all three aspects—musical, documentary, and dramatic—within a single syncretic genre.

A major theme of *The Idea of North* is existential human communion. Ultimately, it is Gould's attempt to communicate on the most serious philosophical level, in a complex, experimental form invented for this purpose; on this level, creation and communication are one. Gould's contrapuntal documentaries, and particularly the philosophical *Solitude Trilogy*, are his greatest creations, the realizations of his desire to move from the world of performance to that of "composition."

Before plunging into *North* itself, it will be useful to offer some background: first, a sketch of the Canadian national institution of CBC radio during its Golden Age; and second, some sense of the North itself, the Canadian archetype that also strongly influenced this production.

CBC radio performed a unique function from the mid-1930s on, fulfilling its legal mandate to preserve Canadian culture and unify the country. In those days, Canada was just emerging from the long-standing cultural colonialism of both Britain and the United States. English Canada had (for example) only a fledgling book-publishing industry, a fledgling film industry, and no real national professional theatre. In the absence of these more traditional instruments of cultural diffusion, CBC radio developed by the 1940s into English Canada's primary national medium for culture and entertainment, and it dominated in these respects until at least the late 1960s, when Gould was creating *North*.

As to the archetype of the North in the Canadian psyche: Gould idealized Canada's North as an escape from our rootless urban civilization, but it could function as such precisely *because* it was a frozen Arctic waste. The Arctic climate can be literally fatal, as the fate of the pioneers of the Northwest Passage shows; it has become the archetype of the great frozen Antagonist of Nature. The American archetype of North is slightly different: it is north of, and related to, the archetype of the tropical American South. To Americans, their North is the series of northernmost states along the Canadian border, from Maine to Washington, while the Canadian North is a *second degree* of North that only *begins* at their own far northern extremity. Canada, the "Great White North," sweeps two thousand miles north from the American border, past sub-Arctic Churchill, Manitoba, on the sixtieth parallel, past the Arctic Circle, as far as the North Pole. Canadians themselves cannot escape this extreme psychological archetype of the Far North—the ultimate Thule. Of course, few Canadians ever go even halfway up Hudson's Bay to Churchill (as Gould did), and fewer yet get to live in the Arctic for any length of time (as the characters in *North* all did). But this makes the North even *more* powerful as an archetype in the Canadian psyche, one that was in the back of Gould's mind when he spoke of the *idea* of North. In his documentary, Gould identifies the North as that antagonistic Nature which Canadians have been confronting for generations, ever since winter decimated our first settlers in the early sixteenth century.

As Gould argued, our North is the haven to which one can escape from the existential angst of urban civilization; it is the solitude in which one can be free, yet in which each is forced to confront himself. One can make oneself whole in that place, and discover a new moral and social grounding. Or fail, and be returned to Nature's frozen bosom. Or flee south and condemn the process to interruption. Gould conceived of the North as the archetype of human isolation, and it is this idea, with its challenge to existential authenticity and communication, that is shared by the three programs of the *Solitude Trilogy*. In *North*, the isolation and the challenge are different for each of Gould's characters, but in the most general sense each is forced to confront the self, and for most of them the confrontation is the prelude to a new sense of self.

The Idea of North was clearly autobiographical for Gould, in the sense of playing out his own development: he abandoned the definition of himself as a stage performer, a definition forced on him by our urban civilization; he left the concert stage and turned inward, to the solitude of the studio, which led him to fulfill his urge to create by means of his contrapuntal documentaries. It is not by chance that after he finally gave up concert performance he was himself irresistibly drawn to the Canadian North, seeking there the solitude and the challenge necessary to complete his own transformation. His thousand-mile railway trip from Winnipeg north to Churchill, in 1965, provided the scene as well as the archetypes for *The Idea of North*. As he described it in his introduction to the 1969 rebroadcast, he spent a whole day of that trip in the dining car, in earnest conversation with retired railway surveying engineer Wally Maclean, experiencing the very same revelations that his characters in *North* offer to the silent newcomer who is their auditor in this dramatic fiction.

Adapted from Howard Fink, "Glenn Gould's Idea of North: The Arctic Archetype and the Creation of a Syncretic Genre," in *Glenn Gould*, vol. 3, no. 2 (Fall 1997), pp. 35–42.

The Idea of North
Glenn Gould

This is Glenn Gould, and this program is called *The Idea of North*. I've long been intrigued by that incredible tapestry of tundra and taiga which constitutes the arctic and subarctic of our country. I've read about it, written about it, and even pulled up my parka once and gone there. Yet like all but a very few Canadians I've had no real experience of the North. I've remained, of necessity, an outsider. And the North has remained for me a convenient place to dream about, spin tall tales about, and, in the end, avoid.

Several years ago I went north aboard a train known affectionately to Westerners as the Muskeg Express—Winnipeg to Fort Churchill—one thousand fifteen miles, two nights, one day, four double bedrooms, eight sections, diner, and coach. And at breakfast I struck up a conversation with one W. V. McLean, or as he was known along the line and at all the hamlet sidings where his bunk car would be parked, Wally. Wally McLean is a surveyor, now retired, and within the first minutes of what proved to be a day-long conversation, he endeavored to persuade me of the metaphorical significance of his profession. He parleyed surveying into a literary tool, even as Jorge Luis Borges manipulates mirrors, and Franz Kafka badgers beetles. And as he did so I began to realize that his relation to a craft, which has as its subject the land, enabled him to read the signs of that land, to find in the most minute measurement a suggestion of the infinite, to encompass the universal within the particular. And so when it came time to organize this program and to correlate the disparate views of our four other guests, I invited Wally McLean to be our narrator and to tell me how, in his view, one can best attain an idea of North.

W. V. MCLEAN:[1]   Well, the only way I see this happening is in an extended ride north. When I say that, I mean a long, terrible, trying trip. Perhaps to Churchill, by way of Thompson, going and coming, past Ilford and Gillam, this long, almost trans-Siberian experience that we now face. And for those that face it perhaps for the first or second or third time there's almost a traumatic experience. They feel awe. This is going to become impossible. It may not be now, but it's going to be. And yet they're able to do little or nothing about it. What finally, you ask, is done about it? Well, here's my guess. What really happens is this: the train is about to leave The Pas, see? And five hundred ten miles away north and east is going to be Churchill a day later. And what does the person do on leaving The Pas? Do you know what happens? He sits there in the day coach — the newsie is just ahead of him — and these people, the conductor and the brakeman and so forth, who are accustomed to this, are sort of making nothing of it.

---

[1] W. V. (Wally) McLean, retired surveyor.

THE IDEA OF NORTH

He sits there wondering, Oh, this is going to be forever. It's already been a day, now it's going to be another day, and what about this one? Before long he's going to have to perhaps say hello and, you know, pass the odd word to his fellow man. And indeed it isn't long before we've heard what he has to say: why, for the first time, he's going north. With what? Well, with the army, with the navy, with the air force, with these initials that he always throws at you—DPW, what's that? Oh, Department of Public Works. With DRNL, what's that? What is it? Defense Research Northern Laboratories? What's that? Well you're studying the Northern Lights, then? Well, well, well. Now you can listen for awhile. Because what do any of us know about the Northern Lights?

MARIANNE SCHROEDER:[2]   I was fascinated by the country as such. I flew north from Churchill to Coral Harbour and Southampton Island at the end of September. Snow had begun to fall, and the country was partially covered by it. Some of the lakes were frozen around the edges but towards the center of the lake you could still see the clear, clear water. And flying over this country you could look down and see various shades of green in the water, and you could see the bottom of the lakes, and it was a most fascinating experience. I remember I was up in the cockpit with the pilot, and I was forever looking

---

2   Marianne Schroeder, nurse.

out left and right. I could see ice floes over Hudson's Bay, and I was always looking for a polar bear or some seals that I could spot. But unfortunately there were none. And as we flew along the east coast of Hudson's Bay, this flat, flat country frightened me.

JAMES LOTZ:[3] Like a large number of people who end up in the North, I got there by mistake. I strayed in there. I think my first attempt to go north was when, during a summer vacation when I was at university in England, I thought about going to Iceland. I'm not too sure why. And instead, because I'd made a mistake about the fare, I ended up in Morocco. I'm a geographer by training, and I have this belief, you see, that geographers are people who have no sense of direction, just as sociologists are people who don't like society, and economists are people who can't really manage their own money. Though some evidence in the North indicates they have a pretty good time with the public purse. I came to Canada after I'd been in West Africa for a year. I came to Canada, again like so many other immigrants, because I couldn't get a job in England. I came to Ottawa to place my services at the disposal of the federal government, and the federal government had other ideas. So after working in a few dead-end jobs in Ottawa—advertising and copywriting and other things—I applied

---

3 James Lotz, geographer.

to McGill and was encouraged to go north to the McGill Subarctic Research Laboratory to do some fieldwork for the thesis. The thesis was on soils and agricultural possibilities in the Knob Lake area, PQ.[4] There isn't a great deal of soil, and as far as I can make out there are no agricultural possibilities. This is what's known as negative evidence in science. And I began to get the impression that the North is a land of very narrow, very thin margins. Man, of course, is a biological improbability at the best of times. If you wanted to design something that could live on this earth, you wouldn't design a man. And in the North, in many respects we're at our greatest and our most grotesque.

WM: Well, is this a surprise? No, it's no surprise at all. The person that makes the trip more often, of course, is going to realize that before long he's going to be up well against himself. Not against his fellow travellers, no, not so much, but he's going to have to be up against his own sad self.

Seems to me that a man by the name of Pascal years back said that most of mankind's troubles would be over with or done away with if he would stay in his own room. At the time I thought this was such a self-evident, banal, silly thing to say that I gave it little thought, but then, on looking back, perhaps

---

[4] Prior to 1991, Canada's official postal abbreviation for Quebec was PQ, short for Province du Québec. —*Analog Sea Editor*

after a few decades, I thought how, indeed, true this is. Can a man get along with himself, usually in this solitary life of the hermit North or the solitary life of any place where he secludes himself?

ROBERT A. PHILLIPS:[5]   I think it takes a strong person to live in the North and really to be a part of it and find satisfaction there. When you're living in a big city in the South you can always retreat when you fail in your relations with society. You can just go away and nobody really knows the difference. You can't go away when you're in a little village and a thousand miles from nowhere and a couple of weeks from the next plane, high in the arctic.

In some ways you may have gone to the North to get away from society, and you find yourself far closer to it than you've ever been in your life. You know your neighbors intimately. You know each walk they take down that little five-hundred-yard road. You know what their problems are because they're bound to talk to you about them. If they don't, they'll go nuts, just as you'll go nuts when you don't talk.

Sometimes you'll find yourself rather pathetically persuading yourself that this is great. And you'll sit on a Saturday night on the kind of couch that you'll see in every village of the North from Baffin Island to the Mackenzie

---

[5] Robert A. Phillips, government official.

Delta. They're all identical in the government houses. And you'll get in a sing-song with the trader and his wife and the priest, or the other missionary, the policeman and so on. You'll sing the same sort of songs whether in Baffin Island or the Mackenzie Delta, and you'll exchange the same gossip about so-and-so who's just moved from this store to that or Doctor so-and-so who's probably coming through on the next flight in ten days and so on. And you convince yourself that this is really the life, that there's a kind of precious intimacy about all this.

JL: I was in many respects solitary, but in a strange way the North has made me more gregarious, because the North does show you exactly how much you rely on your fellow man, what the sense of community means. The sense of community in the North, unlike in the South, is a matter of life and death. The thing about the North of course in personal terms is that in the North you feel it's so big. It's so vast. It's so immense. It cares so little. And this sort of diminishes you, and then you think, My God, I am here. I live here. I live. I breathe. I walk. I laugh. I have companions.

RP: There's a wonderful cliché that a nation is great only as long as it has a frontier. Now we've got that frontier. Other people are nostalgically having to dip back a hundred years to find their frontier and vicariously become part of it. We've got it. And we have a very small percentage of our population who really take advantage of it in the specific physical way, but for a lot of the rest of us it is a sort of frontier in much more than the physical sense. This does something to the Canadian character. It means we've got a kind of civilization that does not conform to the rest of North America. Here is a place where nonconformists can live and flourish. The kind of person who goes to the North is rather odd. And if you're smart, you'll go on looking for this kind of odd person.

WM: There's such a thing as being a hermit by choice rather than being a hermit by necessity. Now it all depends on whether you think you're answering a challenge or escaping from yourself. Are you in fact escaping in any real way by retreating North? Or by retreating perhaps in any direction?

A certain William James—perhaps at the turn of the twentieth century—said that there was no moral equivalent of war. Well, I read that. There is no moral equivalent, said William James. No moral equivalent of war. That is, there's nothing like war for providing something for you to be against. Apparently very few of us can afford to be *for* something. Apparently all of us can afford to be *against* something. All right then, so I can tell this chap, this research chap heading north for Churchill, that we can all be fellow men when we know what we're against. But what are we against in this situation where we're rolling north, these endless miles of steel clickety-clack of the rails, the punctuated monotony of the telegraph wires outside the day coach window? This and that make us at least fellow humans. I almost find it impossible to get this over except to say to this chap who is bound to listen because the miles are bound to stretch out and the night is going to fall endlessly, it seems. There's going to be a little place called Pikwitonei, mile two-fourteen, and he'll wonder why the train is standing this long at that lonely spot, and the darkness of night's going to surround him, and we're going to back up, and he's going to be twice perplexed. And in order to answer his perplexity I'm gonna say, "I suppose the common enemy is Mother Nature." "Oh," he says, "Yes." Cause he's willing now to be a fellow traveler of my imagination, eh? So I go on to say that the North is the war, that you can afford to be against Mother Nature if only humans make it possible. Well, he asks, "What's wrong with that? What's good about that or bad about that?" I say, "There was a time, believe me, in living memory, when humans used to combine against Mother Nature. Not only because they had to, but because, in a sense, there was a cleanness, a sureness, or a definiteness about coming up with Mother Nature that is lacking in our rootless pavements, in our big-city anonymity." You know he shrinks from this, and he's got to listen, though. Remember the train is barely pulling out. How many hours there are left in his mind, I've no idea, but perhaps he hasn't any idea either. But now of course I get into a complaining mood shortly after this. He looks at me questioningly, and my patience perhaps with myself runs out and I say, "Ah yes, but that's the North that *was*." No longer do humans combine to defy, or to measure, or to read, or to understand, or to live with this thing we call Mother Nature. Our number-one enemy, instead of being Mother Nature, is of course *human* nature. It's crept stealthily from the South — not necessarily by steel, all these long and endless miles that we've sort of passed. And now it's infected. It's infecting the North with a contagion that is — huh, I don't know what it's like. I don't dare tell this person that. He's a nice fellow, you know, and I don't want to destroy his dream. Also I don't want to smash my own, which is paper-thin at times. So we're up against this William James that wrote in Harvard this many years ago. I suppose he meant really that the moral equivalent for us is — not war — but going North.

Adapted from a transcript of Glenn Gould, *The Idea of North* (Toronto: CBC Records, 1992). *Solitude Trilogy* is a collection of three hour-long radio documentaries — *The Idea of North* (1967), *The Latecomers* (1969), and *The Quiet in the Land* (1977) — which Gould produced for the Canadian Broadcasting Corporation.

Silence and Solitude
Blaise Pascal

On the occasions when I have considered the various ways men bustle about, and the peril and pain to which they expose themselves at court or in war—sources of so many quarrels, passions, bold and often ill-fated endeavors, etc.—I've often thought that all of humanity's misfortune stems from just one thing: not knowing how to sit quietly in a room. A man with enough to live on, if only he knew how to stay at home happily, wouldn't go away to sea or lay siege to a city. A commission in the army would not cost so much were staying put in town not deemed intolerable; and those seeking conversation and games do so only because they find no pleasure in staying at home.

Blaise Pascal, "Divertissement," in *Pensées: Ed. de 1670* (Paris: Flammarion, 1913), no. 139. First published in French as *Pensées sur la religion et sur quelques autres sujets* in 1670. Excerpt translated by Sarah Ream for Analog Sea.

The Behavior of Light
Barry Lopez

I marveled as much at the behavior of light around the icebergs as I did at their austere, implacable progress through the water. They took their color from the sun, and from the clouds and the water. But they also took their dimensions from the light: the stronger and more direct it was, the greater the contrast upon the surface of the ice, of the ice itself with the sea. And the more finely etched were the dull surfaces of their walls. The bluer the sky, the brighter their outline against it.

I wrote words down for the tints—the grays of doves and pearls, of smoke. Isolated in my binoculars, the high rampart of a mesa-like berg seemed sheared off like a wall of damp talc. Another rounded off smoothly, like a human forehead against the sky, and was pocked and lined, the pattern of a sperm whale's lacerated tun. Floating, orographic landscapes—sections broken out of a mountain range: snow-covered ridges, cirque valleys, sharp peaks. The steep walls often fell sheer to the sea, like granite pitches, their surfaces faceted like raw jade, or coarser, like abraded obsidian.

Where the walls entered the water, the surf pounded them, creating caverns, grottoes, and ice bridges, strengthening an impression of sea cliffs. At the waterline the ice gleamed aquamarine against its own gray-white walls above. Where meltwater had filled cracks or made ponds, the pools and veins were milk-blue, or shaded to brighter marine blues, depending on the thickness of the ice. If the iceberg had recently fractured, its new face glistened greenish blue—the greens in the older, weathered faces were grayer. In twilight the ice took on the colors of the sun: rose, reddish yellows, watered purples, soft pinks. The ice both reflected the light and trapped it within its crystalline corners and edges, where it intensified.

Excerpted from Barry Lopez, *Arctic Dreams* (London: Vintage Classics, 2014), pp. 206–207. First published in 1986.

Rotten Ice
Gretel Ehrlich

The Arctic is shouldering the wounds of the world, wounds that aren't healing. Long ago we exceeded the carrying capacity of the planet, with its seven billion humans all longing for some semblance of first-world comforts. The burgeoning population is incompatible with the natural economy of biological and ecological systems. We have found that our climate models have been too conservative, that the published results of science-by-committee are unable to keep up with the startling responsiveness of Earth to our every footstep. We have to stop pretending that there is a way back to the lush, comfortable, interglacial paradise we left behind so hurriedly in the twentieth century. There are no rules for living on this planet, only consequences. What is needed is an open exchange in which sentience shapes the eye and mind and results in ever-deepening empathy. Beauty and blood and what Ralph Waldo Emerson called "strange sympathies" with otherness would circulate freely in us, and the songs of the bearded seal's ululating mating call, the crack and groan of ancient ice, the Arctic tern's cry, and the robin's evensong would inhabit our vocal cords.

Excerpted from Gretel Ehrlich, "Rotten Ice," *Harper's Magazine* (April 2015), pp. 41–50.

Wunderkammer
Ralph Waldo Emerson

The Universe is a more amazing puzzle than ever as you glance along this bewildering series of animated forms—the hazy butterflies, the carved shells, the birds, beasts, fishes, insects, snakes—and the upheaving principle of life everywhere incipient in the very rock aping organized forms. Not a form so grotesque, so savage, nor so beautiful but is an expression of some property inherent in man the observer—an occult relation between the very scorpion and man. I feel the centipede in me—cayman, carp, eagle, and fox. I am moved by strange sympathies, I say continually "I will be a naturalist."

Excerpted from Ralph Waldo Emerson, *Journals and Miscellaneous Notebooks: 1832–1834*, vol. 4 (Cambridge, MA: Belknap Press of Harvard University Press, 1964), pp. 199–200.

The Lost Pianos of Siberia
Sophy Roberts

I used my search for a piano to discover the story of Siberia. It might sound a little curious—the idea of this bulky musical instrument in the wilds of remote Russia—but there was a logic to it.

In the nineteenth century, "pianomania" exploded in western Russia, in the two cities of Moscow and St. Petersburg. The makers couldn't produce the instruments fast enough to meet demand. As the Tsarist regime strengthened its colonizing impact on Siberia, the piano, which was a great signifier of "Western" culture, went with its emissaries. In *The Lost Pianos of Siberia*,[1] I traced some of these instruments as they moved across the Ural Mountains, which is the edge of Siberia as Chekhov defined it, and out to the frozen reaches of the Pacific coast. The absurdity of an unwieldy instrument in such a formidable place appealed to me.

Some of the earliest examples of keyboard instruments went with the explorers. In the 1730s, Bering's wife, Anna, set off with a clavichord strapped to the back of her sledge—a six-thousand-mile journey to and from the Pacific along a northern route where some of the coldest temperatures on Earth have been recorded. And then you have the Decembrists, the noble revolutionaries of the 1820s who were exiled to

---

1 Sophy Roberts, *Lost Pianos of Siberia* (London: Doubleday, 2020).

Siberia as prisoners to work in the silver mines. Their wives went with them too, the best known of whom was Maria Volkonsky, much admired by Pushkin and, later, Tolstoy. I love the fact that, reduced to bare essentials, she crossed a frozen Lake Baikal in winter with a clavichord. The solace music brought her is reflected in a painting by a fellow prisoner which depicts her in the labor prison with her husband, the clavichord beside her. Later, when their incarceration was over, the Decembrists had to remain within Siberian territory. Maria's brother sent her a Lichtenthal; this grand piano survives today in the city of Irkutsk, where Maria had an enormous influence on musical culture, even opening a concert hall. This is just one of the many strands of the story of Siberia's fascinating relationship with the piano, which also flowered in the Soviet period, when music became open to all.

In his book, *The Hare with Amber Eyes*, Edmund de Waal writes, "Objects have always been carried, sold, bartered, stolen, retrieved and lost. People have always given gifts. It is how you tell their stories that matters."[2] I took heart from this when writing my book. When I knocked on doors in the back of beyond in Siberia and said, "I'm an English woman, it's minus twenty outside, and I'm looking for a piano," their stories suddenly opened up around a common passion. Infusing

---

2 Edmund de Waal, *The Hare with Amber Eyes: A Hidden Inheritance* (Chatto & Windus, 2010), p. 402.

these pianos were remarkable stories about human endurance, lost love, and the comfort that these instruments (sometimes grossly out of tune) were still able to communicate.

Siberia conceals so many stories both sad and uplifting about our species' capacity for cruelty and beauty. The Gulag narrative was difficult to write. I struggled. Often it felt like I was walking on bones and ghosts, a trespassing outsider. Of the stories that stuck with me, one was that of French-born concert pianist Vera Lotar-Shevchenko, whose last piano I uncovered. When she ended up in a Soviet Gulag in the Ural Mountains, the female prisoners saw how badly she pined for her piano. Apparently, they carved a keyboard into her wooden bunk with a kitchen knife so that she could practice silently at night. Another account instead gives her Gulag piano as a kitchen table. Where the stories converge, though, is in 1950: the first thing Vera did on her release was to walk through the local town to find a music school. Still wearing her convict's quilted pea coat, she asked to play the piano.

Vera sat at that instrument for one, maybe two hours— there are others who say far longer. She played without stopping, laughing and crying, the recall of her repertoire note-perfect as her stubby fingers behaved with the same exhilarating precision as they had before her arrest. Teachers and students who were listening at the door were dumbfounded by this magnificent squall of Chopin, Liszt, and Beethoven. It was as if every part of her being were lost to the power of music.

You and Art
William Stafford

Your exact errors make a music
that nobody hears.
Your straying feet find the great dance,
walking alone.
And you live on a world where stumbling
always leads home.

Year after year fits over your face—
when there was youth, your talent
was youth;
later, you find your way by touch
where moss redeems the stone;

And you discover where music begins
before it makes any sound,
far in the mountains where canyons go
still as the always-falling, ever-new flakes of snow.

Advice to a Graduation
Glenn Gould

I know that in accepting the role of advice-giver to a graduation, I am acceding to a venerable tradition. However, it's a role that rather frightens me, partly because it's new to me, and partly because I'm firmly persuaded that much more harm than good accrues to gratuitous advice. I know that on these occasions it is customary for the advice-giver to tell you something of the world that you will face—based, of course, upon his experience—one that necessarily could not duplicate that which may be your own. I know also that it is customary to recommend to you the solutions that have proved themselves valid within the speaker's experience, sometimes to dish them up anecdotally in the "When I was your age"—or, even more mischievously, in the "If I were your age"—tradition. But I have had to reject this approach, because I am compelled to realize that the separateness of our experience limits the usefulness of any practical advice that I could offer you. Indeed, if I could find one phrase that would sum up my wishes for you on this occasion, I think it would be devoted to convincing you of the futility of living too much by the advice of others.

What can I say to you that will not contravene this conviction? There is, perhaps, one thing which does not contradict my feeling about the futility of advice in such a circumstance as this, because it is not based upon calling to your observation something demonstrable—that is to say, something that need

ADVICE TO A GRADUATION

be demonstrated and hence will most likely be rejected—but is simply a suggestion about the perspective in which you view those facts that you possess already and those which you shall subsequently choose to acquire.

It is this: that you should never cease to be aware that all aspects of the learning you have acquired, and will acquire, are possible because of their relationship with negation—with that which is not, or which appears not to be. The most impressive thing about man, perhaps the one thing that excuses him of all his idiocy and brutality, is the fact that he has invented the concept of that which does not exist. "Invented" is perhaps not quite the right word—perhaps "acquired" or "assumed" would be more acceptable—but "invented," to return to it, somehow expresses more forcefully, if not quite accurately, the achievement that is involved in providing for an explanation for mankind, an antithesis involved with that which mankind is not. The ability to portray ourselves in terms of those things which are antithetical to our own experience is what allows us not just a mathematical measure of the world in which we live (though without the negative we would not go far in mathematics) but also a philosophical measure of ourselves; it allows us a frame within which to define those things which we regard as positive acts. That frame can represent many things. It can represent restraint. It can represent a shelter from all of those antithetical directions pursued by the world outside ourselves—directions which may have consistency and validity elsewhere but from which our experience seeks protection. That frame can represent a most arbitrary tariff against those purely artificial but totally necessary systems which we construct in order to govern ourselves—our social selves, our moral selves, our artistic selves, if you will. The implication of the negative in our lives reduces by comparison every other concept that man has toyed with in the history of thought. It is the concept which seeks to make us better—to provide us with structures within which our thought can function—while at the same time it concedes our frailty, the need that we have for this barricade behind which the uncertainty, the fragility, the tentativeness of our systems can look for logic.

You are about to enter—as they say on these fearsome occasions—the world of music. And music, as you know, is a most unscientific science, a most unsubstantial substance. No one has ever really fully explained to us many of the primevally obvious things about music. No one has really explained to us why we call high "high" and low "low." Anyone can manage to explain to us what we call high and what we call low; but to articulate the reasons why this most unscientific, unsubstantial thing that we call music moves us as it does, and affects us as deeply as it can, is something that no one has ever achieved. And the more one thinks about the perfectly astonishing phenomenon that music is, the more one realizes how much of its operation is the product of the purely

ADVICE TO A GRADUATION

artificial construction of systematic thought. Don't misunderstand me: when I say "artificial" I don't mean something that is bad. I mean simply something that is not necessarily natural, and "necessarily" takes care of the provision that in infinity it might turn out to have been natural after all. But so far as we can know, the artificiality of system is the only thing that provides for music a measure of our reaction to it.

Is it possible, then, that this reaction is also simulated? Perhaps it, too, is artificial. Perhaps this is what the whole complicated lexicon of music education is meant to do—just to cultivate reaction to a certain set of symbolic events in sound. And not real events producing real reactions, but simulated events and simulated reactions. Perhaps, like Pavlov's dogs, we get chills when we recognize a suspended thirteenth, we grow cozy with the resolving dominant seventh, precisely because we know that's what is expected of us, precisely because we've been educated to these reactions. Perhaps it's because we've grown impressed with our own ability to react. Perhaps there's nothing more to it than that we've found favor with ourselves—that the whole exercise of music is a demonstration of reflex operation.

The problem begins when one forgets the artificiality of it all, when one neglects to pay homage to those designations that to our minds—to our reflex senses, perhaps—make of music an analyzable commodity. The trouble begins when we start to be so impressed by the strategies of our systematized thought that we forget that it does relate to an obverse, that it is hewn from negation, that it is but very small security against the void of negation which surrounds it. And when that happens, when we forget these things, all sorts of mechanical failures begin to disrupt the function of human personality. When people who practice an art like music become captives of those positive assumptions of system, when they forget to credit that happening against negation which system is, and when they become disrespectful of the immensity of negation compared to system—then they put themselves out of reach of that replenishment of invention upon which creative ideas depend, because invention is, in fact, a cautious dipping into the negation that lies outside system from a position firmly ensconced in system.

Most of you at some time or other will engage in teaching some aspect of music, I should imagine, and it is in that role that you are most liable, I think, to what I might call the dangers of positive thinking.

I am, perhaps, in no position to talk about teaching. It is something that I have never done and do not imagine that I shall ever have the courage to do. It strikes me as involving a most awesome responsibility which I should prefer to avoid. Nevertheless, most of you will probably face that responsibility at some time; and from the sidelines, then, it would seem to me that your success as teachers would very much depend upon the degree to which the singularity, the uniqueness, of the confrontation between yourselves and each one of your students is permitted to determine your approach to them. The moment that boredom, or fatigue, the *ennui* of the passing years, overcomes the specific ingenuity with which you apply yourself to every problem, then you will be menaced by that over-reliance upon the susceptible positive attributes of system.

You may remember the introduction that George Bernard Shaw supplied to his collected writings as music critic, and in which he describes an early ambition to develop the native resonance of his baritone and grace the stages of the world's opera houses. He was encouraged in this, apparently, by a lively charlatan, one of those walking fossils of music theory, who already had ensnared Shaw's mother as student and who proclaimed himself in possession of something called "the Method." It seems that after several months' exposure to the Method, Bernard Shaw took to his typewriter and was never able to carry a tune again.

I do not, for one moment, suggest that you minimize the importance of dogmatic theory. I do not suggest, either, that you extend your investigative powers to such purpose that you compromise your own comforting faith in the systems by which you have been taught and to which you remain responsive. But I do suggest that you take care to recall often that the systems by which we organize our thinking, and in which we attempt to pass on that thinking to the generations that follow, represent what you might think of as a foreground of activity—of positive, convinced, self-reliant action—and that this foreground can have validity only insofar as it attempts to impose credibility on that vast background acreage of human possibility that has not yet been organized.

Those of you who will become performers and composers will not perhaps be quite so vulnerable, if only because the market in which you will have to operate is insatiably demanding of new ideas, or, at any rate, of new variations upon old ideas. Furthermore, as performer or composer you will in all likelihood exist—or, at any rate, should try to exist—more for yourself and of yourself than is possible for your colleagues in musical pedagogy. You will not be as constantly exposed to the sort of questions which tempt ready answers from you. You will not have quite so great an opportunity to allow your concepts of music to become inflexible. But this solitude that you can acquire and should cultivate, this opportunity for contemplation of which you should take advantage, will be useful to you only insofar as you can substitute for those questions posed by the student for the teacher, questions posed by yourself for yourself. You must try to discover how high your tolerance is for the questions you ask of yourself. You must try to recognize that point beyond which the creative exploration—questions that extend your vision of your world—extends beyond the point of tolerance and paralyzes the imagination by confronting it with too much possibility, too much speculative opportunity. To keep the practical issues

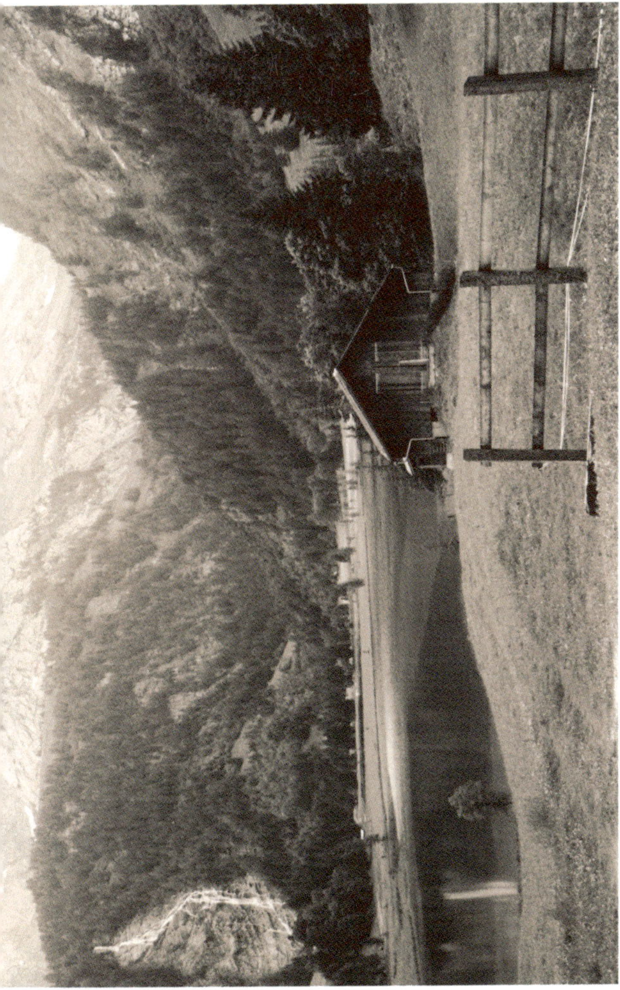

Analog Sea

Dear Reader,

So you managed to find us amid all the flickering and noise. Thank you for that, and for supporting your local bookstores and writers.

If you discover something valuable in this work, please tell other daydreamers about Analog Sea, our books, our biannual journal, *The Analog Sea Review,* and our wish for a little slowness now and then.

And if you want to stay in touch, to receive our seasonal bulletins and other mailings, why not send us a letter? Be sure to include your name, mailing address, and perhaps what was happening when you first discovered the Analog Sea.

Poems, drawings, and other outpourings of solitude are always welcome.

Yours truly,
Analog Sea

Basler Strasse 115
79115 Freiburg

PO Box 11670
Austin, TX 78711

ADVICE TO A GRADUATION

of systematized thought and the speculative opportunities of the creative instinct in balance will be the most difficult and most important undertaking of your lives in music.

Somehow, I cannot help thinking of something that happened to me when I was thirteen or fourteen. I haven't forgotten that I prohibited myself anecdotes for tonight. But this one does seem to me to bear on what we've been discussing, and since I have always felt it to have been a determining moment in my own reaction to music, and since anyway I am growing old and nostalgic, you will have to hear me out. I happened to be practicing at the piano one day—I clearly recall, not that it matters, that it was a fugue by Mozart, K. 394, for those of you who play it too—and suddenly a vacuum cleaner started up just beside the instrument. Well, the result was that in the louder passages, this luminously diatonic music in which Mozart deliberately imitates the technique of Sebastian Bach became surrounded with a halo of vibrato, rather the effect that you might get if you sang in the bathtub with both ears full of water and shook your head from side to side all at once. And in the softer passages I couldn't hear any sound that I was making at all. I could feel, of course—I could sense the tactile relation with the keyboard, which is replete with its own kind of acoustical associations, and I could imagine what I was doing, but I couldn't actually hear it. But the strange thing was that all of it suddenly sounded better than it had without the vacuum cleaner, and those parts which I couldn't actually hear sounded best of all. Well, for years thereafter, and still today, if I am in a great hurry to acquire an imprint of some new score on my mind, I simulate the effect of the vacuum cleaner by placing some totally contrary noises as close to the instrument as I can. It doesn't matter what noise, really—TV Westerns, Beatles records; anything loud will suffice—because what I managed to learn through the accidental coming together of Mozart and the vacuum cleaner was that the inner ear of the imagination is very much more powerful a stimulant than is any amount of outward observation.

You don't have to duplicate the eccentricity of my experiment to prove this true. You will find it to be true, I think, so long as you remain deeply involved with the processes of your own imagination—not as alternative to what seems to be the reality of outward observation, not even as supplement to positive action and acquisition, because that's not the way in which the imagination can serve you best. What it can do is to serve as a sort of no man's land between that foreground of system and dogma, of positive action, for which you have been trained, and that vast background of immense possibility, of negation, which you must constantly examine, and to which you must never forget to pay homage as the source from which all creative ideas come.

A full transcription of Glenn Gould's commencement address delivered at the Royal Conservatory of Music, University of Toronto, November 1964.

At the Blue Note
Pablo Medina

Sometimes in the heat of the snow
you want to cry out

for pleasure or pain like a bell.
And you wind up holding each other,

listening to the in-between
despite the abyss at the edge of the table.

Hell. Mulgrew Miller plays like a big
bad spider, hands on fire, the piano

trembling like crystal,
the taste and smell of a forest under water.

The bartender made us a drink
with butterfly wings and electric wire.

Bitter cold outside, big silence,
a whale growing inside us.

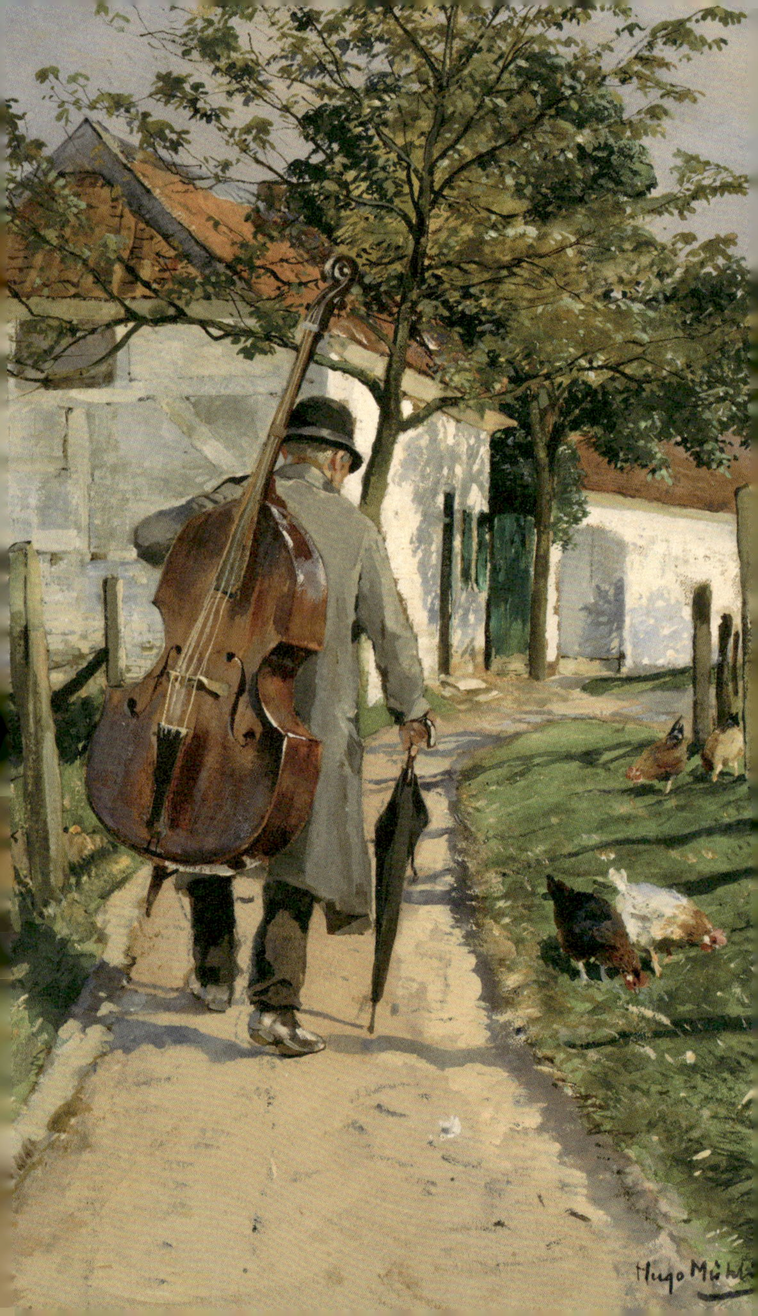

Tangier Syndrome
Simon-Pierre Hamelin

I am described as a writer, publisher, and bookseller in Tangier, but that is not the full story. I am the unwitting custodian of a slender-columned temple where divinities of different languages and civilizations are worshiped. In the morning I flick a feather duster over our idols, framed photographs of writers—true icons. In reverential silence I get ready to open the shop on the Boulevard, one of the principal stations of the Tangier pilgrimage. Above all else, this is a literary city, the like of which is rare. It is one of the last sanctuaries for poets and dreamers.

There is nothing fusty or strictly regulated about these matinal rites. The veneration of Literature that we are almost the last in the world to practice in this archaic manner is an ancient and joyous religion, without the customary austerity. It is more an art of living, a response to the increasing stupidity of humans. Elsewhere, all the gods are dead. In Tangier, writers are our deities.

I am the guardian of a little shrine perched above the metropolis that dominates the Strait of Gibraltar. Our chapel stands on Tangier's *decumanus maximus*, its main thoroughfare, Boulevard Pasteur, known simply as "the Boulevard," as if it were the only one. Its promenade, the Terrasse des Paresseux—the idlers' terrace—affords an unparalleled view.

According to oral tradition, our earliest literature, this was the first land after the Flood. Legend has it that after drifting for forty days and forty nights in search of *terra firma*, when Noah saw a dove returning to the Ark with mud on its feet, the cry that went up was "*Tin jaa!*"—the land has returned. Tangier, first land; Tangier, the birthplace of literature.

The city's storied origin is closely bound up with the beginnings of universal literature through its association with Homer, Plato, Strabo, and others. Tangier and its region are the backdrop for some of Hercules' labors. Ulysses reached our westernmost extremity, where he confronted the Cyclops and laid the foundations of our literary mythology—one that is still alive today. The giant Antaeus, whose tempestuous love affairs are chronicled in *The Iliad*, was the son of Gaea and Poseidon, fruit of the earth and the sea. In the Greek and Berber traditions, he is the founder of our city, and is said to be buried beneath the tree-covered Charf Hill, which is visible from the Bay of Tangier. Hercules, his victor, smashed through Mount Atlas to reach the Garden of the Hesperides, thus creating the Strait of Gibraltar. He then established a vast cave sanctuary on Cape Spartel, where the Atlantic meets the Mediterranean. The Caves of Hercules still exist and have been a tourist attraction ever since Truman Capote held an extravagant birthday bash there in the 1950s.

I am the scrivener of the Boulevard whose job is to preserve the memory, oral and written, nurture the mythology, shape the legend, annotate the gospel, and assist the hordes of pilgrims who come from around the globe. The Garden of the Hesperides is supposedly a few miles from Tangier on the ancient site of Lixus, overlooking the meandering river that flows into the ocean. No golden apples are to be found here now, only ancient olive trees.

In the distance lies the coastal town of Larache, where two great writers of the twentieth century, Jean Genet and Juan Goytisolo, rest side by side in a hilltop cemetery. Goytisolo, a very dear friend, departed this world in 2017. They too are heroes of our times, or rather saints; in any case Genet was. The bad boy of French literature is known here as Sidi Gini, literally Saint Genet, and his name is suffused in legends and attested miracles. Overlooking the Atlantic between a former brothel and a prison, rituals—the nature of which I shall not reveal—are performed on his grave. Juan, his neighbor, also a cursed child of Literature, has not been resting there long enough to have been canonized. But this will come about in time because here we are well practiced at creating heroes in the ancient mold. Their attributes are paper, ink, the pen, and the raised fist.

I am a Pythian priestess of this modern-day Babel where all tongues can be heard depending on the speaker's mood and which way the wind is blowing, where we are obliged to speak all languages, even badly. The oracles are pronounced in the dialects of the entire known world. That of Tangier itself is a variation of Arabic inflected with Berber, Spanish, and French. On any one day, I will speak Arabic, French, and English, with a smattering of German or Italian. I will converse with my grocer in Russian and with fans of Bollywood movies in Hindi.

Literature in Tangier was born before Babel. It is universal, with the emphasis on rhythm and music, whatever the language. We have our way of the cross, our holy stations, our saints, our heroes, our daily carnival of eccentric, colorful figures, our actors, our make-believe settings, our illusionists, and our numerous pilgrims who come to watch this curious spectacle without always understanding its value and uniqueness.

Our most venerable literary figure is that of an explorer, Ibn Battuta, a native of Tangier. After having journeyed seventy-five thousand miles, he dictated his travel tales to the poet Ibn Juzayy al-Kalbi, whom he met in Granada in the mid-fourteenth century, at a time when crossing the Strait and traveling the world was less impeded by walls and borders than nowadays. His wanderings took him as far as the edges of China, where he taught Islam, and it is to him we owe the first poetic account of this far-flung East.

Cantonese entrepreneurs, who are playing an active part in the development of the city of Tangier and its great port, can be seen searching for the tomb of the explorer-poet. Roaming the streets of the medina, cell phone in hand, they seek out the miniature dome capping the tomb attributed to Tangier's first writer. We keep the location of his grave as secret as possible, so that each can find their own path through the labyrinthine medina. And when some come and complain to me that they have been unable to locate the tiny, hidden mausoleum, I can only reply politely (for you must not upset a pilgrim) that they must be patient, that things of value have to be earned, because it is the quest that is truly important, just like the long journey of this son of Tangier.

I am the Brahmin of a shimmering temple where people come from all four corners of the earth to pay tribute to William Burroughs, Allen Ginsberg, and Jack Kerouac, and to indulge in hashish and other substances. So thin and hollow-cheeked that he was dubbed the invisible man, Burroughs wrote *Naked Lunch* in one of the rooms of the Hotel Muniria—another of the stations of our pilgrimage. It was Ginsberg who assembled the novel after gathering up the precious pages from the floor amid an unspeakable shambles.

Setting sail from New York, and even before arriving in Tangier, Burroughs had banged away frenetically on his typewriter to the pounding of the waves. The path was well trodden since Paul Bowles had moved there in the 1940s on the advice of Gertrude Stein, who held court in Paris. Bowles, the musician turned writer, which in Tangier are one and the same thing, was the most venerated literary idol of the city on the Strait and the reluctant godfather of that generation which he neither appreciated nor understood but preferred to mock.

Bowles was a genius inventor. He recognized the talent of our greatest contemporary writer, Mohamed Choukri, who learned to read and write Arabic at the age of twenty and asked Bowles to translate into English his masterpiece, *For Bread Alone*, which was banned in Morocco for some twenty years. Choukri became an icon as greatly admired as Bowles. Similarly, Paul Bowles harnessed the magical imagination of Mohamed Mrabet, an illiterate writer and brilliant storyteller, for whom the American author was the pen for more than thirty years. Bowles unveiled the Mediterranean oral literature that Mrabet brought to life, combining it with anecdotes from contemporary Tangier. Bowles died in 1999, leaving Mrabet without a scribe, and two of us took up the torch. I transcribed several of his texts—in true Tangier fashion, in Arabic, Spanish, and French, and with the help of gesticulations—including *Manaraf*, a genre-defying novel published in the Netherlands which draws on episodes from Mrabet's own life mixed with ancient legends of the city and the history of the Rif mountains. It centers on a cast of traditional characters (fishermen, crooks, talking fish) and the artists and writers Mrabet met in the company of Bowles—for whom he was cook, driver, and storyteller for forty years—including Truman Capote, Francis Bacon, Tennessee Williams, William Burroughs.

I am one of the soldiers of the battalion of Letters. Our struggle is both poetic and political. Our weapons are paper, our flagship the Librairie des Colonnes bookstore. It is where our secret army of partisans was founded in 1949 by Robert Gerofi, a Belgian archeologist who corresponded with André Gide and was curator of the Museum of the Kasbah, an architect, and an art teacher. He was such a fervent admirer of Marguerite Yourcenar and her novel *Memoirs of Hadrian* that he sailed across the Atlantic aboard the yacht of his friend Malcom Forbes to present the writer with a ring which was set with a coin engraved with the likeness of the Roman emperor. The artefact had been unearthed at the archaeological site of Lixus, the famous Garden of the Hesperides. She wore it all her life.

Anti-Franco and pro-feminist ahead of its time, the bookstore was run by Robert's sister and his wife, the Gerofi ladies. Jean Genet used to come to pick up his royalties sent by Gallimard; Tennessee Williams and Truman Capote would meet up there; Jane and Paul Bowles used it as a postal address; Choukri came to borrow books; Mrabet exhibited his phantasmagorical paintings and drawings and always dropped in once a week to say hello to the staff.

Our battle is to bring books and wonderment to places where they are not, and to continue enchanting people. Our enemies are greedy traders, car culture and touch-screens, all pencil pushers, and the smooth-talkers in thrall to modern dictatorships of the mind.

I am the watchman of a day hospital, an open-air hospice, welcoming, in this city where there is only one pathology, those suffering from Tangier syndrome. The Librairie des

Colonnes is the waiting room, even though there are no consultations. Besides, there is no cure.

Tangier syndrome is a variation of Jerusalem syndrome, which affected many nineteenth-century writers during their stay in the holy city, and is nowadays erroneously referred to as "culture shock." In Jerusalem, travelers began exhibiting eccentric behaviors stemming from the fantasies they had superimposed onto Biblical characters and the city, the cradle, of course, of the three monotheistic religions. Fantasies that came up against a very different reality, leading to self-denial, the invention of a new identity, the overturning of all values.

Tangier syndrome is somewhat different in that its obsessions have a chiefly literary focus. The primary pathology, which in my view is rather an art of living, is self-reinvention. It is a veritable manufacture of larger-than-life characters, total fabrications created by the cheery victims of this syndrome. That is where the invisible boundary between creative genius and madness lies; they go hand in hand.

I am the shaman of the Librairie des Colonnes, and I listen unperturbed to the many and comical victims of our syndrome. In particular a young man by the name of Proust who speaks contemptuously of Marcel and presents himself as the only true writer of the family—to which this young man most likely does not belong. But what does it matter? He boasts that he has been working for ten years on a *roman-fleuve* of which no one has yet been able to read a word. He is invited by all

TANGIER SYNDROME

the literati of Tangier because he plays the part to perfection. In Tangier, it is enough to declare oneself a writer, painter, filmmaker, or whatever one dreams of being, for it to come true. Unfortunately, no distinction is made between those who genuinely write or paint and those who are simply indulging in self-reinvention. To exist beyond the fantasy, "authentic artists" must remain hidden and never appear on the dangerous stage where illustrations of the syndrome are played. And very fortunately, those working in secret and in silence are numerous. Rachida Madani is a poet whose work is political and profound. She writes in anonymous cafés and at the table at night when her children are asleep. She has been translated into English and is one of our most beautiful Tangier voices. Likewise, François-Olivier Rousseau, whose precise and precious pen I admire, has managed to remain incognito in this den of artifice and games. He never comes to the bookstore for fear of bumping into pilgrims or the actors of our Tangier stage.

Among the cohort of artists are playwrights, because while Tangier is a literary city, it is also a city of theater. Zoubeir Ben Bouchta writes plays often inspired by Tangier legends and Tangier syndrome. Since Tennessee Williams' sojourn in Tangier, American theater has also featured. One of Williams' young Broadway assistants, Joe McPhillips, lived in Tangier in the 1960s alongside his close friend, the writer John Hopkins. For thirty-five years, McPhillips was head of the American School, which was one of the last humanist schools of the

Mediterranean. Until he left us in 2007, each year the school would put on a play with young actors who were pupils at the school. A brilliant director, McPhillips asked Tennessee Williams to write a play (*Camino Real*), calling upon Yves Saint Laurent to design the costumes, Paul Bowles to compose the music, and Allen Ginsberg to do the actors' make-up. He directed some twenty plays in this manner, performed twice a year without any video recordings.

McPhillips was my closest friend. He was the person who made me a writer by forcing me—and rightly so—to read the most sacred works of literature, by teaching me to listen just to Bach, who was for him the only song of the angels.

I am the custodian of the temple, a follower of the sect of Literature. I visit the graves of the dead, our idols. As people do in Russia, I regularly spend several hours at the tombs of Choukri, Genet, Goytisolo, and McPhillips. I offer libations, pouring a little vodka on their tombstones. I raise my glass with them, I recite a poem like a prayer, a mantra that we alone understand. I talk with them a little and continue the story; I write in the hope that this harmony will never end and that Tangier will remain this tremendous and sacred paradise, as it was and will be from the beginning until the end of the world.

Translated from French by Ros Schwartz for Analog Sea.

Poetas del Mundo
Jonathan Davidson

England is far away from the center of world poetry, which, I discovered a few years ago, is Nicaragua. In this small Central American country with a turbulent recent history, poetry is important. Nicaragua may not be any better or worse for its involvement with poetry, but poetry is at the heart of the country in a way that it might once have been in England. Andrew Marvell and John Milton would have recognized some aspects of Nicaragua in the 1970s.[1] The poetry, war, and revolution that transformed that country in the twentieth century were peculiarly English things in the seventeenth. They deposed a dictator; we executed a king. Spending even a short period of time in Nicaragua, as I did a few years ago, changed my view of what poetry might do in the world. It did this by allowing me not just to experience a celebration of poetry inextricably bound to politics but by hearing English as it is for millions of people—a little language possibly on its last legs.

In February 2014 I found myself as one of twenty people in a shallow boat propelled at speed across a lake.[2] Around us were other boats on the same journey and still more would

---

[1] Poets and politics, basically.

[2] Lake Nicaragua, one of very few lakes in the world to have freshwater sharks.

follow, carrying perhaps one hundred *poetas del mundo*[3] and a few relatives and friends. The waters were calm but ran deep. Some people were wise-cracking in Spanish, others stared into the middle distance. As we approached an island we heard the familiar sound of the little brass band that had accompanied our every move for days. They played jaunty tunes and made us feel special. And here they were again. It was the last of the seven days of the Festival Internacional de Poesía de Granada in Nicaragua, and we had relaxed into our roles. Language united us and divided us, although the one-fifth of the poets who didn't speak Spanish were still diligently attending every reading, soaking up the sound, if not the sense. We were clearly out of our depth but determined to enjoy the experience. We had found enough fellowship from across the seventy-one countries represented to feel that although we were not at the center of this world, we were in orbit around it.

So much of my poetry life had, up until this point, been concerned with the minutiae of putting poetry into the world —how to pronounce correctly the Scottish towns featured in W.S. Graham's poetry, learning the words of poems by heart, attending to every beat in the bar—and here I was suddenly at the other end of the spectrum, at a festival that seemed to concern itself very little with details but simply stood four-square in the world's way and got itself noticed. Quite possibly there

---

[3] Poets of the world!

are other poetry festivals that effortlessly take over a small city, but Festival Internacional de Poesía de Granada was like nothing I had ever attended. It took the aspirations and practicalities of presenting poetry in the UK and did exactly the opposite.[4] It was simply good sense. With a climate like Nicaragua's, no one is going to hunt out the back room of a pub or a local library. The poetry readings were outdoors in the evenings and in most cases presented in Granada's city square, in front of the Cathedral, making the poetry visible and public. It would have been impossible to sell tickets in such a setting, so goodbye box-office income. The practicalities would have defeated the most diligent of venue managers and, more to the point, in Nicaragua, for all its divisions and inequality, poetry is for the people. While the guest poets and dignitaries sat in reserved seats close to the stage, the rest of the audience were packed tightly around them, sitting and standing, motionless and milling around. They were free to come and go. They came and went.

Having a free event in the center of a city is not usually a *guarantee* of audiences, but here it seemed to be. It was helped by the fact that after every poetry reading (and these lasted up to three hours) there would be a popular singer or a well-known band performing—but people were certainly there for the poetry. The poetry, by the Latin American poets at

---

[4] I believe this was their motto: "Let us do it as the English would not."

least, was spoken calmly and quietly, while the amplification flung it into the night sky. If something can be amplified, the Nicaraguans will amplify it. The parakeets are noisy, and the ice-cream sellers ring their bells incessantly, but poetry must be heard. And poetry must be seen as well, so there were two large screens either side of the stage. The northern European convention of quiet poetry, quietly spoken in quiet places to small audiences, would have seemed ridiculous here. The poets did speak quietly, but their quietness was made loud. The audience's concentration was palpable. There were no corners cut when it came to making sure everyone heard every word. This was quite a responsibility for the poets, for their voices to fill a city square full of attentive strangers. No one was going to give applause if it had not been earned.

The poets I read alongside demonstrated how to read poetry the Latin American way. Their approach was to have confidence in the words, to cut out the chit-chat, to make no apology, and at no point try to entertain the crowd. That would have been undignified. They had dignity. In the course of the Festival, across dozens of hours of poetry, I did not hear a single indication of enjoyment from the audience other than the applause that followed concentration. Even the nodding of heads and murmurings of appreciation at the end of the poem, the default response of UK audiences, was absent. This was not, to resort to the hollow phrase beloved of poetry-event promoters in the Anglo-sphere, a place of entertainment. But still they stayed, the audiences. Stayed and listened. Listened then applauded.

The Festival that year was in honor of Nicaragua's national poet, Rubén Darío (1867–1916). It transpired that everyone in Nicaragua, and most poetry readers across Latin America, knew his work. As my Nicaraguan poet friend, Francisco Larios, explained, Darío was such a well-known and well-loved writer, so important for the self-respect of the country, that every Nicaraguan child with even the remotest interest in writing — and that was many, it seemed — wanted to be the next Rubén Darío.[5] In his lifetime Darío immersed himself in the world, active as a poet and writer, but also a diplomat and traveler, as at home in London or Madrid as in Granada or Managua. In Nicaragua, as the Festival demonstrated, there was a belief that if a man or woman (but sadly, still far too often a man) could write fine poetry, then it followed that their intellect would be of use in the wider world, that they could possibly see more clearly what needed to be done, that they were more understanding of the frailties of our fellow citizens and therefore better able to rise above and to represent the people, all of the people.

I am very likely romanticizing a festival, a writing culture and a country that I do not well enough understand. However,

---

[5] His poetry was available in the airport bookshop in Managua. And not only his poetry, but lots of other poetry, in Spanish and English. Heathrow it was not.

one of the guest poets—in this case a special guest—had certainly found himself as a writer unable to retire to his *chaise longue* with a bottle of absinthe and a delicate constitution. Ernesto Cardenal was a Catholic priest and a published poet who found himself increasingly at odds with the regime of the Somoza family in the Nicaragua of the 1960s and 1970s. In his efforts to defend the poor and powerless he became a leading figure in the revolution led by the Sandinistas. His earlier poetry wasn't written with an expectation of a public, but he responded to the revolution by writing long, detailed documentary poems, to explain and record what was really going on in a form that, thanks to the efforts of Darío and others, would be appreciated by a wide cross-section of the population, and certainly not just the literate and educated. Poets are eminently peripatetic, but poetry is even more so. A good poem can move across a country—memorized, recited, referenced—at a speed to outflank even a well-equipped repressive regime. And of course, unlike ordinances, decrees, declarations, and the Riot Act, poetry takes strength from speaking between the lines, from saying one thing and meaning another, from coming up behind figures of authority.

In Cardenal's case, he believed that poetry could at least *help* make something happen. He was like Brecht in that respect. And when the revolution had started he stayed to try to see things through, joining the government, serving as their first Minister of Culture from 1979 to 1987. He could have stepped back into the literary shadows. He didn't. Inevitably, as a politician, he fell out with others, and not everything went well, but when many years later he read his poems at the Festival, a rather frail old man with an Old Testament beard and the obligatory revolutionary's beret, the silence was reverential. He was an example of poetry applied to life.

Cardenal's reading was part of a typical session at the Festival Internacional de Poesía de Granada, which would last up to three hours and feature as many as twenty-five poets, each reading only two or three poems. We formed a temporary poets' commune, and in this spirit there was no sense of anyone being a headline act.[6] The most vivid expression of this egalitarianism was in the carnival, a parade through the city of Granada lasting four hours with poets reading from a platform on the back of a pick-up truck at every corner—amplified of course—to crowds of thousands packed into the narrow streets that stretched down to the lake.

Towns in the northern hemisphere have plenty of parades and singing and dancing, but this was different because the attraction—along with bands and troupes of dancers—was actually the poets, shambling, perspiring, confused group though we often were. They cheered the poets of the world. And to remind us that there are battles still to be fought

---

6 Although the American poet Rita Dove was the non-Nicaraguan special guest, a great poet, and, with her husband, an excellent dancer, both Latin and ballroom.

and that poets should take up their pens to change things, the Festival that year had a focus on women's rights, and at the head of the carnival procession was a horse-drawn hearse carrying a coffin in which we were to collectively bury violence against women and girls by casting it off into the lake. The reading on the following night was by women poets, a gesture towards equality, although regrettably the old male poets still outnumbered the women poets in the Festival.

I had spent the best part of my reading life carving into the granite several hundred names to provide the hand- and toe-holds necessary for me to clamber about the cliff face of poetry. But despite my interest in those who were relatively unknown, the geomorphology I had created was Anglocentric. In Nicaragua in the space of a week I was covering the globe with the gold stars of the poets I had met, and South and Central America glittered. I was still rooted in the British Isles, but my center of gravity was edging offshore. Within a few days of hearing so much poetry in Spanish and in so many other languages, English was starting to sound rather quaint. It was strange but not unpleasant, pale and potentially interesting, a language that didn't get out much.

Before being translated into Spanish, poets read in their own languages, including Estonian and Hebrew and French and German and Arabic, so it was possible to start to hear how their languages offered differences and similarities. There may have been abstruse references and the subtleties of local color, but first there was the music of the dancing syllables. With sufficient time a poem in Portuguese echoes a poem in Finnish, and mostly, unexpectedly, it was the revealed silences that gave them kinship. It is, after all, the silences that create whatever shadow poetry casts. The spaces in which we wait and think.

Where Are the Intellectuals?
Alberto Manguel

During the Argentine military dictatorship of the seventies, faced with atrocities that had seemed inconceivable until a decade earlier, a number of writers attempted to analyze and denounce the events they were witnessing. Theirs were not only punctual denunciations but also well-thought-out reflections on the nature of state-sanctioned violence and the moral corruption underlying official discourse. On March 24, 1977, Rodolfo Walsh, fiction writer and investigative journalist, published an open letter to the military Junta blaming them for "the fifteen thousand disappeared, the ten thousand unjustly imprisoned, the four thousand dead, the tens of thousands forced into exile." Walsh's letter ended with these words: "These are the thoughts that on the first anniversary of your unhappy government I've wished to address to the members of this Junta, without hope of being heard, certain of being persecuted, but faithful to the engagement I assumed long ago of bearing witness in troubled times."

That was forty years ago, and the "troubled times" have changed protagonists and plots, but they have not come to an end. Every day the news reports countless atrocious events and, in a number of countries (Russia, Syria, Turkey, Venezuela, China) journalists and writers are being jailed, tortured and sometimes killed for making these events public. But in many other countries, especially in those where the government disguises its atrocities under the cover of seemingly democratic procedures, occasional reporting and snippets of political speeches are not enough. Where, in our so-called democracies, are the clear, coherent, irrefutably critical voices of our age, not merely denouncing but reasoning in depth the causes of these atrocities? Paul Nizan, in the 1932 essay *Les Chiens de guard*, denounced the silence of many of the thinkers of his time. "The gap between their thought and a universe plagued by catastrophe widens every week, every day, and they are oblivious." And he added, "All those foolish enough to have waited for their words begin to revolt, or to laugh."[1]

Since at least the days of ancient Athens, to bear witness in troubled times is considered a citizen's duty, part of a civic responsibility in maintaining a more or less well-balanced society. To the laws and regulations of officialdom, the individual must constantly oppose questions: it is in the tension (or dialogue) between what is ordered from the throne and what is objected to from the street that a society must exist. This civilian activity, which Marx, in his 1845 "Theses on Feuerbach,"[2] called a "practical-critical" activity, is what Walsh saw as the defining role of the intellectual.

---

[1] Paul Nizan, *Les Chiens de guard* (Paris: Maspero, 1965), p. 121. First published in 1932. Excerpt translated by Analog Sea.

[2] First published posthumously in German as an appendix to Friedrich Engels, *Ludwig Feuerbach* (Stuttgart: J.H.W. Dietz, 1888).

Since antiquity then, the intellectual has assumed such a role in every society we have established. Whether claiming a professional fee, like the Sophists, for entering "the public market of ideas," or merely for love of truth and justice like Socrates; whether against the strictures of the Church or the abuses of the State; whether honored by one's fellow citizens or vilified and persecuted for one's public statements, the intellectual has at almost all times taken on the function of society's critical voice. Certain historians have noted that the modern persona of the intellectual was born during the protests of the mid nineteenth-century in Tsarist Russia, as a member of the intelligentsia; others have found its roots in the Dreyfusards led by Émile Zola in nineteenth-century France; yet others find the origins of the public intellectual in the writers of the Enlightenment, such as Locke, Voltaire, Rousseau, and Diderot.

This role, however, is not the exclusive prerogative of recognized writers such Zola and Locke: every individual human being must be capable of thinking universally. Sometimes, the notable intellectual is Everyman who does not possess what we could call a professional voice. These men and women might be (and usually are) unconscious of their assumed role as ordinary people speaking from an ethical core, naturally critical witnesses of their time. Here Antonio Gramsci's observation is useful: "There is no human activity," he wrote in his

"Cuaderno 12,"[3] "from which one can exclude all intellectual intervention; one cannot separate *Homo faber* from *Homo sapiens*."[4] Every *Homo sapiens* can, at certain moments, stand up and speak for all those condemned to remain anonymous. Shortly before the events of May '68, Edward Said defined the intellectual in these clear terms: "The intellectual, as I understand it, is not a peacemaker nor a builder of consensus, but someone who engages and risks his entire being based on a constantly critical sense, someone who refuses at whatever cost simple formulas, ready-made ideas, complacent confirmations of the statements and actions of those in power and other conventional minds."[5]

What we need right now is engaged intellectuals speaking loud and clear about our present suicidal situation. We need

---

3 Antonio Gramsci, "Cuaderno 12 (XXIX): Apuntes y notas para un grupo de ensayos sobre la historia de los intelectuales," [Notebook 12 (XXIX): Notes for essay about the history of intellectuals] in *Cuadernos de la cárcel: Edición crítica del Instituto Gramsci*, ed. Valentino Gerratana, trans. Ana María Palos (Mexico City: Ediciones Era, 1981), p. 382. First published in Italian as *Quaderni del carcere* in 1975.

4 "There is no human activity from which one can exclude all intellectual intervention; one cannot separate *Homo faber* from *Homo sapiens*. In short, every man outside his profession explains a certain intellectual activity, is a 'philosopher,' an artist, a man of taste, participates in a conception of the world, has a line of conscious moral conduct, therefore contributes to sustain or modify a conception of the world, that is to say, to raise new ways of thinking." Translated from Spanish by Analog Sea.

5 Edward Said, *Des intellectuels et du Pouvoir* (Paris: Seuil, 1996).

to be reminded, day after day and night after night, that the essence of Utopia is its inexistence, and that the responsibility of intellectuals is not to dream up plans for a utopian society that will never come about but to speak up in order to improve the society we have now, shakily rooted on this earth. This can be achieved, at least in part, by holding up the mirror of the world to all of us who inhabit it and shaming us into action. *New York Times* journalist Charles Blow asked his fellow Americans in a recent editorial: "Where were you when the bodies floated in the Rio Grande? What did you say when this president bragged about assaulting women and defended men accused of doing the same? What was your reaction when he saw very good people among the Nazis? Where was your outrage when thousands died in Puerto Rico? What did you do? What did you say? And for others in my profession, what did you write?"[6]

Perhaps they are here, but we do not yet hear their voices clearly nor see their real stature. Perhaps, being their contemporaries, we are too close to them, and it requires the distance of a century or two to identify the Voltaires and Socrates of today. Added to this disadvantage of proximity, we suffer today from another, more grievous one that dims these voices, wherever, as we trust, they exist.

The twenty-first century is the age of disbelief in the word. Almost for the first time in history, the instrument

---

[6] Charles Blow, "It's the Cruelty, Stupid," the *New York Times* (July 3, 2019).

of language is not generally considered as an instrument of reason that allows us to assess and transmit experience in as precise a way as possible. Ambiguity, uncertainty, approximation have always been features of our language, but in spite of these frailties (which poets convert in strengths) we have been able to come up with crutches to uphold sense and meaning, such as tone and grammar and countless rhetorical devices, and these have worked more or less effectively up to now. But today, public discourse seems to rely almost exclusively on the conveyance of emotion, and incoherence is seen not as weakness of thought but as proof of authenticity, of something that comes not from the cold workings of a rational mind but something sincere, gushing forth "from the gut." A tweet or a commercial slogan carry today more weight than a carefully pondered essay. In this climate of unreason, the intellectual act loses its ancestral prestige, and, as we know all too well, fake news and public lies are allowed to prevail. Intellectuals are depicted by those in power as "enemies of the people" set against the ordinary citizen whom they are accused of despising. It is therefore more urgent and more important that, amidst these accusations of negligence and superciliousness, reasonable voices, voices like that of Rodolfo Walsh in the past, steadfastly bear witness. There are no excuses for intellectual indecision.

Before the Gates of Hell, Dante sees the swarm of the Undecided whom Hell rejects and Paradise does not want, rushing around in circles, pursued by gadflies and wasps. "This miserable way," Virgil tells him, "is taken by the sorry souls of those / who lived without disgrace and without praise."[7] We must choose, and the choice with which every intellectual is confronted is whether or not to be a critical witness of our cruel times: to look and see the fate of the weak, the powerless, those who have been denied a voice, those banished into oblivion washed up on the coast of Lampedusa or the banks of the Rio Grande. But also, to engage in reasoned argument with those in whose hands lie the strategic decisions that decide the fate of those bereft of a rightful voice. In short, the undeniable choice is whether or not to speak.

---

7 Dante Alighieri, *The Divine Comedy of Dante Alighieri: Inferno*, trans. Allen Mandelbaum (New York: Bantam, 1982), Canto III, 34–36. Completed in 1320 and first published in Italian as *La commedia* in 1472.

In Dark Times
Bertolt Brecht

They will not say: when the nut tree shook in the wind
But rather: it was when the housepainter trampled the workers
They will not say: when the child skimmed the flat pebble over the rapids
But rather: when the ground was being prepared for great wars.
They will not say: when the woman walked into the room
But rather: when the great powers united against the workers.
But they will not say: the times were dark
But rather: why were their poets silent?

Translated from German by David Constantine and Tom Kuhn.

The Vienna of Yesterday
George Prochnik

There's a historical anecdote that illustrates how the act of cultivating funds of imaginative aptitude can work against the oppressive consciousness of defeat in such a way as to enable an entire city to recreate itself in the wake of catastrophe.

In 1940, two years after Adolf Hitler annexed Austria to Germany and just months before the fall of France, the Viennese writer Stefan Zweig delivered a lecture in Paris titled "The Vienna of Yesterday." The speech is laced throughout with poignant observations about the city's cosmopolitan and ethnically and religiously diverse heritage. But perhaps its most original passage comprises a fervent defense of the arts as a seedbed for ideas and skills that might one day rescue civilization—even though they should be practiced with no knowledge of or concern for potential real-world applications.

Zweig writes of Vienna's long, distinguished history of devotion to the arts, music, and theater in particular. He describes the almost fanatical dedication of Austrian performers and composers to their trade—as well as the intensely passionate attention of Viennese audiences to these virtuoso exhibitions. How the Germans used to ridicule the Austrians for their frivolous pastimes! Zweig exclaims. The Austrians were considered pathetically ignorant about how to be productive, just as they were viewed as useless when it came to understanding how to prevail on the battlefield or in business. They had, indeed, no meaningful quantifiable knowledge whatsoever. "For the German people," Zweig wrote, "the concept of '*jouissance*' is always linked to effort, activity, success, to victory. To be fully himself, each must outstrip his neighbor and if possible oppress him." Instead of this philosophy, the Austrians had cultivated the idea that "one must be free and leave others to their freedom," without being ashamed of "taking pleasure in existence," finding and creating beauty—daydreaming about other worlds.

So far as the Germans were concerned, the Viennese lack of knowledge about the transactional, zero-sum workings of reality doomed the Austrian Empire to absolute irrelevancy.

And yet, Zweig declared, in truth, at the end of the First World War, when Vienna lay in ruins, with grass growing in its streets and all the roads leading to the provinces from where the capital drew its resources cut off—when the trains were without coal, and the shops were empty of bread, fruit, or meat, and the currency was becoming devalued by the hour—all that supposedly idle, feckless immersion in the pursuit of aesthetic joy proved to have another dimension, which the Viennese themselves had been unaware of until that time. For, Zweig argued, it was precisely all those countless hours spent practicing the arts and handicrafts that gave the city's residents the skills and imagination necessary to resurrect a city that war and disease had virtually annihilated.

"The miracle happened," Zweig wrote: in three years everything had been rebuilt. In five years, the city had constructed blocks of communal houses that became the model of successful socialist governance for all of Europe. Commerce resumed. Galleries and gardens were restored. "Vienna became more beautiful than ever before," and suddenly found itself at the forefront in a hundred vital areas.

In Zweig's vision, the art of the imagination, to which the city had accorded primacy, gave the population faith that the apocalyptic scenes before them were as impermanent as stage sets. And the conviction that these sights could be transformed came in tandem with an understanding of how the transformation could be effected which went beyond what might be derived from any rigid manuals of pragmatic knowledge.

Saving Vienna
Stefan Zweig

And that is how, through a fanaticism for art, a passion so often ridiculed, we once more saved Vienna. Expelled from the top rank of nations, we nevertheless retained our place at the heart of European culture. The mission to defend a higher culture against all forms of barbarism, the mission that the Romans engraved into our very walls—we fulfilled it right up to the final hour.

We fulfilled it in the Vienna of yesterday, and we shall continue to fulfill it abroad and everywhere. I spoke of the Vienna of yesterday, the Vienna where I was born and where I lived and which I love today more than ever now that I have lost it. […] Art and culture cannot prosper without freedom, and the culture of Vienna cannot flourish if it is cut off from the vital source of European civilization. The mighty struggle that today shakes our world will definitively decide the fate of this culture, and I hardly need tell you on which side my most ardent wishes lie.

Excerpted from the lecture "Das Wien von Gestern" [The Vienna of Yesterday], which Stefan Zweig gave in Paris in April 1940. First published in Stefan Zweig, *Zeit und Welt. Gesammelte Aufsätze und Vorträge* 1904–1940, ed. Richard Friedenthal (Stockholm: Bermann-Fischer, 1943). Translated from German by Will Stone.

Light for a Cold Land
Arthur Erickson

I was sixteen when I met Lawren Harris[1] and his wife Bess, and they were to change my life. A close family friend, Nan Cheney, the artist and intimate of Emily Carr, brought the Harrises to see my art work. I anticipated the visit with great excitement and remember vividly when they walked up the path to my parents' house how imposing he was—erect, trim, vital, with that corona of white hair framing soft but lively brown eyes and the beautiful Bess at his side. Her beauty emanated not only from startling sky-blue eyes but from the grace that pervaded her manner, her gestures, her voice, and what it said. Devoted, radiant, each shone in the other's presence.

Lawren's "at home" Saturday evenings were an astonishing exposure to the purveyors of ideas of his city. Intellectuals not only from Vancouver but also from Europe frequented those evenings, for many composers and conductors, dancers, and writers had come to Canada from the conflagration in Europe. Barbirolli, Britten, Arthur Benjamin, and Sir Ernest MacMillan were a few I remember. Locally the Adaskins, Ira Dilworth, the Binnings, Birneys, Bells, Smiths, Andrews, and MacKenzies were frequent attendees. The ritual was set.

---

[1] Lawren Stewart Harris (1885–1970) was a Canadian artist and one of the Group of Seven landscape painters.

After arriving at eight sharp you were seated in the living room; Lawren selected the first recording of his huge collection, spoke about it, clipped the bamboo needle, turned out the lights and left you in the dark to concentrate only on your aural senses.

At ten the lights went on, and coffee was served. Suddenly from the night of aural enchantment we entered the day of visible light—the silvery light of Lawren's mountain experiences. The clear blues, muted purples, whites, chrome yellows, and silver greys of his non-objective compositions on the walls extended into the serene surroundings of the house. A grey-purple carpet ran throughout on which white or silvery rugs were set with cabinets of beaten tin from Mexico and low white sofas. Lawren's and a few of Bess's paintings glowed with the suffused illumination of the Arctic ice, the mountain summits, the floating icons in an unlimited sky. In this exalted ambience the conversation often turned to Madame Blavatsky, W.Q. Judge, Annie Besant, Buddhism, and theosophy. At that young and searching age I was entranced by the lofty concepts, for they counterbalanced the awful concurrent violence in Europe that I would have to face in another year. The discussions put the tyrannical tendencies of mankind into a more benign cast of human fate, making them less ominous and disillusioning for one beginning a life's adventure.

Vancouver at that time had a population of two hundred thousand, and its cultural life was tenuously centered on the university, symphony, Player's Club, and a small art gallery showing only local works. Lawren changed all that. He awakened the city to its own creative forces in art and music, encouraging the many extraordinary artists, intellects, and patrons of that golden age of Vancouver's youth. Under him the gallery was extended and opened to international shows. By collecting the unknown Emily Carr's work he gave the gallery its only important collection other than his own works. Iby Koerner's courageous Vancouver Festival and Ira Dilworth's pioneering CBC were engendered by the status he had given the arts. You felt you were at the hub of the western creative vortex—leaving Toronto and Montreal far behind. It was one of those rare exhilarating moments in the life of a city in which anything seemed possible.

This Heavy Craft
P. K. Page

The wax has melted
but the dream of flight
persists.
I, Icarus, though grounded
in my flesh
have one bright section in me
where a bird
night after starry night
while I'm asleep
unfolds its phantom wings
and practices.

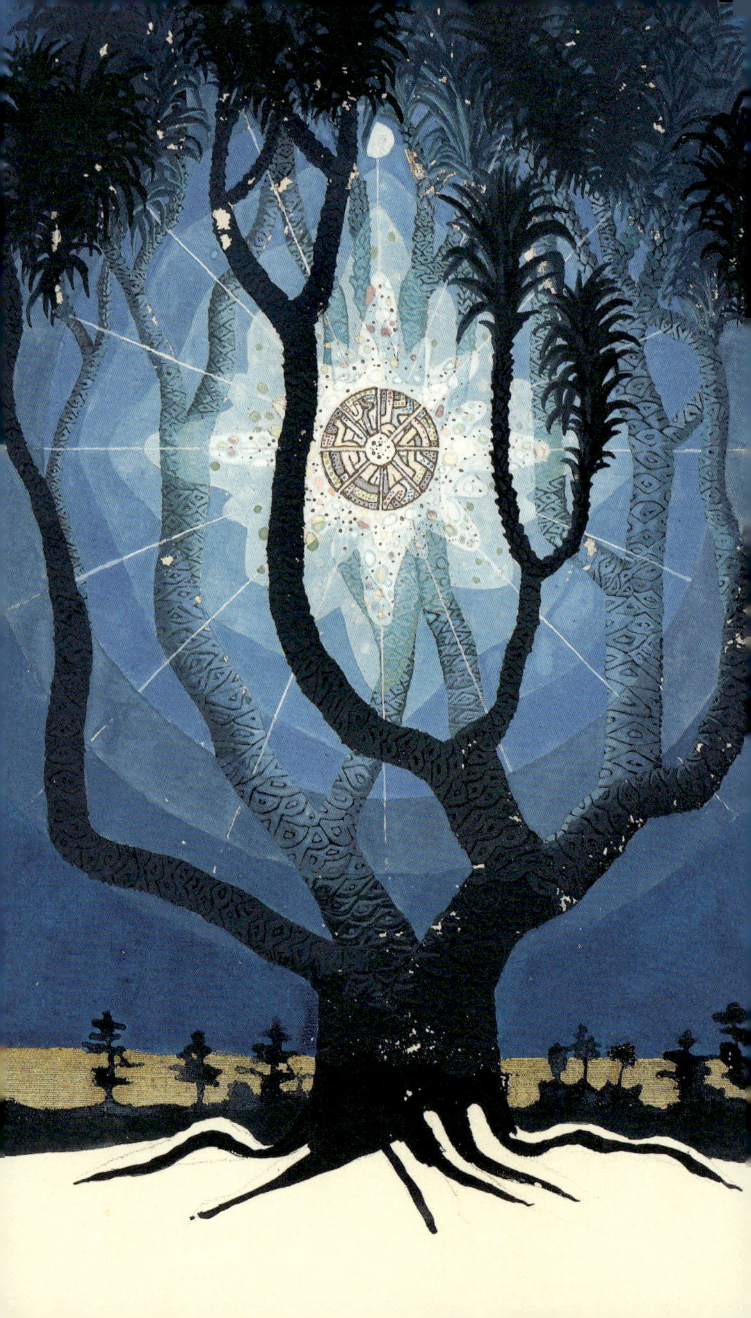

Where It All Began
C.G. Jung

The years, of which I have spoken to you, when I pursued the inner images, were the most important time of my life. Everything else is to be derived from this. It began at that time, and the later details hardly matter anymore. My entire life consisted in elaborating what had burst forth from the unconscious and flooded me like an enigmatic stream and threatened to break me. That was the stuff and material for more than only one life. Everything later was merely the outer classification, the scientific elaboration, and the integration into life. But the numinous beginning, which contained everything, was then.

Foreword to C.G. Jung, *The Red Book*, ed. Sonu Shamdasani, trans. Mark Kyburz, John Peck, and Sonu Shamdasani (London: W.W. Norton & Company Ltd., 2009).

Interview with Andrés Ocazionez
Jonathan Simons

Navigating the leafy, tattered streets of Neukölln, the southeastern borough of Berlin once controlled by American forces, I make my way to a quiet room in an old factory building where Andrés Ocazionez spends his days writing, reading, thinking, and listening to others. A Jungian analyst and scholar, Ocazionez was born in Colombia, did much of his research in Madrid, and completed his analyst training at Carl Jung's original institute near Zurich. After several decades of meeting a myriad of people in quiet rooms, he has garnered a special interest in what makes us human, what makes us suffer, and what makes us delve deeper into this beautiful mess we call humanity.

JONATHAN SIMONS: Perhaps we could begin by attempting to sketch out a basic definition of what we mean by depth psychology?

ANDRÉS OCAZIONEZ: I don't see depth psychology as an alternative to our reality, but rather as a way of getting to its heart. Psychological work is inevitably chained to the real. It's bound to it. I'm reminded of descriptions of the *anima* as going beyond natural experience yet remaining connected to nature—a butterfly flying very close to flowers, or a mist floating over a pond at night. What I read in these images is that the *anima* clearly belongs to its own alien world, yet, at the same time, remains close to our known world.[1] I see something similar in depth-psychological work. Psychology may open new perspectives, often stranger or even deeper than the ones we know; yet these perspectives do not come out of the blue or from the psychologist's need to offer an alternate reality, but rather from the heart of the matter at hand. In my understanding, psychology does not provide depth of its own accord, but it may attempt to go deep into things, or to see things from below, to *under*stand them, so to speak. I don't think that psychology is a cure for the world, much less an alternative to it. Like the *anima*, we always fly very close to the ground; reality is where we start from.

But before working with the real, psychology needs to make it approachable. Alchemy refers to the initial matter from which alchemical work begins as *prima materia*. But first this material needs to be cleaned up a bit, brought into the lab and prepared. In a similar way, strictly speaking, the reality we actually work with in psychology is more of a *secuna materia*, although the alterations are minimal, mostly connected to setting. It is still from this reality, from this world, that we begin, and it is in this world that we remain.

---

[1] Also referred to as analytical psychology, Jungian psychology originated from the work of Swiss psychologist and psychiatrist, C.G. Jung (1875–1961). Jung termed the unconscious, feminine nature of men the *anima* and its opposite in women the *animus*.

JS: Psychology is sometimes seen as a science. But you're referring to the invisible. And when you describe this psychological work, you often employ poetic metaphor. Are we bound to poetry to describe the experience of this work?

AO: Psychology is indeed sometimes considered to be a science, although I don't see it as such. Psychology and science have very different ways of approaching both the invisible and the visible world.

I'm sure that we are not bound to poetry, and nor is poetic language our only option in psychology. But I find that using metaphors opens up a lot of possibilities in my work, especially when it comes to seemingly impenetrable or enigmatic phenomena such as dreams and certain symptoms. I prefer to find ways of echoing or resonating with these types of situations instead of reaching for ready-made interpretations. Metaphor offers a way for me to actively engage with a situation without forcing it to change into something else or solve it too quickly—that is, before its time.

In fact, metaphor may even intensify the situation, or compound the enigma, as James Hillman once put it.[2] Poetic

---

2 "By virtue of their inconceivability, their enigmatic and ambiguous nature, these metaphorical premises elude every literalness, so that the primary urge of seeing through everything fixed, posited, and defined begins archetypally in these fictional premises themselves. Here I am seeking to ground possibility in the impossible, searching for a way to account for the unknown in the still

language is often a form of flight, but it can also be a way of actually getting closer to the essence of things. I remember that Jung once wrote that the best we can do with psychic phenomena is to retell them as well as we can. Now, I don't see myself as a poet, and I don't think that psychology is a kind of poetry, but it may be that both poetry and psychology share the possibility of getting to the heart of the matter linguistically, maybe even lovingly.

JS: How do we transcend intellect and move from the *idea* of something to direct experience? People often see psychology as a very rational practice, as if the ego can somehow illuminate itself, but your work does not seem to me merely an application of ideas. And Giegerich certainly argues that over-intellectualization in depth psychology can lead to its existence as a set of ideas rather than experiences. To me, *depth experience* is one of the best ways to describe what we mean by *interiority*. What do you think?

AO: This is a most interesting topic. I often encounter something curious in my work with patients, or in my dream groups, or while doing research. I would describe it as a

---

more unknown, *ignotum per ignotius*. Rather than explain I would complicate, rather than define I would compound, rather than resolve I would confirm the enigma." James Hillman, *Re-Visioning Psychology* (New York: Harper & Row, 1975), p. 152.

persistent encounter with the *afterwardness* that seems to be an integral part of psychic phenomena.

To give you an example, when I work with dreams, I don't get the feeling that I am working directly with some sort of original pure dream. It seems to me that when we remember a dream for the first time, something of it has been inevitably altered. And when we write it down, the same feeling returns: something else has happened to it. And once again when we tell it to our analyst. You see, direct experience is very elusive in this kind of work. Instead, there's the feeling that we are working within after-experiences: reflections, shadows, echoes, memories, innumerable imperceptible alterations. However, and this is most interesting: in remembering, writing down, and talking about the dream, I don't get the sense of drifting away from it either, but of actually getting closer to it. This gives me the impression that the heart of psychic phenomena, their principle, depth, or *raison d'être*, lies not in a hypothetical beginning but in this *afterwardness*. As the French say, *l'appétit vient en mangeant*.[3]

In fact, that hypothetical original, or pure, dream might *already* be the idea or reflection or illustration of something else. So, it is difficult to know if we can ever move beyond an idea of something. But I don't see this as a shortcoming. I don't see ideas as dead cognitive objects floating around us. Ideas,

---

3 Appetite comes with eating.

like the other aftereffects that I mentioned, may very well be the lifeblood of the soul. And like no other psychologist that I know of, Wolfgang Giegerich is able to articulate this crucial aspect of depth psychology.

JS: So if we describe something as having depth, it must bear more qualities than we can immediately grasp. For instance, if something has a very deep taste, you may not experience all of the subtle notes and flavors immediately.

AO: That's good, yes. And we can put this another way, too: the fact that we cannot immediately grasp or even intuit these other qualities, these other flavors or subtle notes, does not mean that there is no depth to what we are tasting. Jung offers excellent examples of this from his own work with, for example, schizophrenia, and later on with dreams and alchemical texts. Jung was very honest about not understanding the meaning of some things, but he didn't conclude that those things therefore lacked depth or psychological value. He said rather that this was due to his own dullness or lack of understanding. Instead of discarding these phenomena, he stayed with them and, sometimes, the phenomena would reveal their own depth to him. One can also see this in Freud and how he could uncover the most interesting things about even the pettiest of symptoms; this is what he called the psychopathology of everyday life. A certain tolerance to not knowing goes hand in hand with depth in psychological work.

JS: Could falling in love be talked about as potential depth experience? One might say, "It feels like I'm discovering a whole new level of depth, because this other person has all these different stories and energies—entire mountain ranges of feeling that I am just barely able to perceive."

AO: Yes, there might be something about love that requires us not to know, or at least not to know too directly or immediately. Maybe if we knew our lovers too well, we wouldn't love them. Maybe if we knew all the flavors from the outset, we wouldn't be compelled to taste new things. I don't know. I do think that in depth psychology we often find ourselves in a maze of mirrors, of reflections; we often feel we are not seeing the whole picture. But not experiencing everything is not necessarily a disadvantage; it may be an integral part of the experience itself.

JS: Encountering one's limitation or blindness is profound because you realize that every day is a new adventure in a body with senses. I think of Robert Bly and the title of his poetry collection *The Light around the Body*.[4] In spite of the Agrarian,

---

[4] Robert Bly, *The Light Around the Body* (New York: Harper & Row, 1967).

Copernican, Industrial, and Digital Revolutions, there remains so much uncharted territory, so much basic human experience which is ungraspable and cannot be documented or commodified—such as, for instance, amazement at the fact that there is an exploding star above us and light around the body.

AO: Very beautiful. And this is why I like the way you talk about love: there's something very deep about not needing to experience too much. I don't think that depth psychology is necessarily about experiencing new things, deep as they may be.

The French filmmaker Vincent Moon has a recent film called *Híbridos*.[5] He films rituals. He takes his time, and there's no comment, no explanation. You're just faced with the rawness of the ritual. I like this a lot because the filmmaker doesn't seem to me to be interested in taking the viewer on a trip of self-discovery or in satisfying a greed for experiences. Some of the scenes are very long. The viewer may even get bored. You're seeing the otherness of ritual and the fact that it might not be about you. I like this.

JS: So perhaps the purpose of depth psychology—although it's probably not even a good idea to try to package it in this

---

5 *Híbridos: The Spirits of Brazil*, directed by Vincent Moon and Priscilla Telmon (Rio de Janeiro and Paris: Petites Planètes, 2018), DCP, 90 minutes.

way—is, like art, or even Buddhist meditation, that it has no intellectual purpose?

AO: I would add that it might not need an experiential purpose. But I agree, it's not a good idea to package depth psychology in this way, even to say that its purpose is to have no purpose.

There are many things that are of therapeutic value that may have to do with experience—the experience of being understood or of feeling a repressed emotion for the first time, for example, or of having an insight. All of these things are very important for therapy. But I think that when it comes to depth psychology, one has a foot in another plane, a plane beyond direct experience.

JS: As long as the individual has at least some capacity for interiority.

AO: I think so, yes.

JS: Giegerich mentions how, in English, we often translate Jung's notion of *soul* as *psyche* because it sounds more scientific. Do you think we have a soul or souls?

AO: I cannot know. But what I do think is that one can work with soul.

JS: What do you mean?

AO: Jung advocated a psychology *with* soul, which is very different from a psychology *about* the soul. In my understanding, the point of Jungian psychology is not so much to work with the soul as an Other before us, but rather that psychology itself should become as soulful as the contents we are working with. So there is a way of working with psychic phenomena that is not entirely positivistic. This is inevitable anyway, since psychology is merely the extension, echo, or continuation of the psychic content that we are working with. The resonance provided by psychology may open up enough space and time for the phenomenon to unfold of its own accord. Allowing the space for that to happen might be a very rough and incomplete description of what it is to work with soul.

JS: Do you find that interiority is becoming rarer and externalization more extreme? For example, historically, you had the marketplace, which offered a very worldly experience, and then there was your home, which was utterly free of the stress and worries of the marketplace. But now you have a substantial portion of society that's connected to this worldly experience all the time, constantly pulling us outside of ourselves. There's no theoretical reason why introspection, contemplation, and interiority are antithetical to screens, yet, in the end, these states of mind don't seem to coexist well with our digital habits. The constant vying for attention and persistent spectacle of it all engenders externalization. So do you think we are building a society devoid of interiority? And if so, does that make depth psychology obsolete or more necessary than ever?

AO: You ask a very interesting question. What do you think?

JS: I think it's both obsolete and necessary simultaneously. Certain conditions are required for us to continue to enjoy some sort of psychological or spiritual harvest, notably sufficient faculties of attention. I wonder also about emotional wakefulness, empathy for oneself, curiosity. Do you agree some of these conditions are necessary?

AO: Yes. In many ways, I think that what is required is a very antique craft—sitting down with someone, listening to each other, taking time with dreams. Now the machines dream for us, remember for us, have sexual fantasies for us, and all of it is uploaded. But there are still some people sitting on wooden chairs together, talking, taking their time. Some days I feel that this is a kind of privilege, as if there are still a few bottles of a very good wine left. Each time that I have a conversation like this, each time I sit with someone like you and explore these ideas, I think, "Okay, this one is very good. I don't know how long we're going to be able to enjoy this, but we still have our glasses."

Confrontation with the Unconscious
C.G. Jung

At first it was the negative aspect of the anima that most impressed me. I felt a little awed by her. It was like the feeling of an invisible presence in the room. Then a new idea came to me: in putting down all this material for analysis I was in effect writing letters to the anima, that is, to a part of myself with a different viewpoint from my conscious one. I got remarks of an unusual and unexpected character. I was like a patient in analysis with a ghost and a woman! Every evening I wrote very conscientiously, for I thought if I did not write, there would be no way for the anima to get at my fantasies. Also, by writing them out I gave her no chance to twist them into intrigues. There is a tremendous difference between intending to tell something and actually telling it. In order to be as honest as possible with myself, I wrote everything down very carefully, following the old Greek maxim: "Give away all that thou hast, then shalt thou receive."

It is of course ironical that I, a psychiatrist, should at almost every step of my experiment have run into the same psychic material which is the stuff of psychosis and is found in the insane. This is the fund of unconscious images which fatally confuse the mental patient. But it is also the matrix of a mythopoeic imagination which has vanished from our rational age. Though such imagination is present everywhere, it is both tabooed and dreaded, so that it even appears to be a risky experiment or a questionable adventure to entrust oneself to the uncertain path that leads into the depths of the unconscious. It is considered the path of error, of equivocation and misunderstanding. I am reminded of Goethe's words in Part One of *Faust*: "Now let me dare to open wide the gate / Past which men's steps have ever flinching trod." The second part of *Faust*, too, was more than a literary exercise. It is a link in the *Aurea Catena*[1] which has existed from the beginnings of philosophical alchemy and Gnosticism down to Nietzsche's *Zarathustra*. Unpopular, ambiguous, and dangerous, it is a voyage of discovery to the other pole of the world.

---

[1] The Golden (or Homeric) Chain in alchemy is the series of great wise men, beginning with Hermes Trismegistus, which links Earth with heaven.

The Disenchantment of the World
Morris Berman

It was the achievement of Carl Jung first to decipher the symbols of alchemy by means of clinical material from dream analysis, and then on this basis to formulate the argument that alchemy was, in essence, a map of the human unconscious. Central to Jungian psychology is the concept of "individuation," the process whereby a person discovers and evolves his self, as opposed to his ego. The ego is a persona, a mask created and demanded by everyday social interaction, and, as such, it constitutes the center of our conscious life, our understanding of ourselves through the eyes of others. The self, on the other hand, is our true center, our awareness of ourselves without outside interference, and it is developed by bringing the conscious and unconscious parts of our mind into harmony. Dream analysis is one way of achieving this harmony. We can unlock our dream symbols and then act on the messages of our dreams in waking life, which in turn begins to alter our dreams.

But how to analyze our dreams? They are frequently cryptic, and so often violate causal sequence as to border on gibberish. But it is precisely here, Jung discovered, that alchemy can make a crucial contribution. In fact, it is by something like the doctrine of signatures that we are able to figure out what our dreams mean.

The language of alchemy, as well as of dreams, follows a type of reasoning which I have termed "dialectical," as opposed to the critical reason characteristic of rational, or scientific, thought.[1] As we saw earlier, Descartes regarded dreams as perverse because they violated the principle of noncontradiction. But this violation is not arbitrary; rather, it emerges from a paradigm of its own, one that could well be called alchemical. This paradigm has as a central tenet the notion that reality is paradoxical, that things and their opposites are closely related, that attachment and resistance have the same root. We know this on an intuitive level already, for we speak of love-hate relationships, recognize that what frightens us is most likely to liberate us, and become suspicious if someone accused of wrongdoing protests his or her innocence too hotly. In short, a thing *can* both be and not be at the same time, and as Jung, Freud, and apparently the alchemists all understood, it usually is.

Within the context of the alchemical paradigm, it is critical reason that appears meaningless, and actually rather stupid, in its attempt to rob significant images of their meaning. Thus, if I dream that I am my father and that I am arguing with him, it is irrelevant that this is not logically or empirically

---

[1] I am following the terminology used by Norman O. Brown in *Life Against Death* (Middletown, CT.: Wesleyan University Press, 1970). First published in 1959. For an interesting discussion of the language of dreams, see Ann Faraday, *The Dream Game* (New York: Perennial Library, 1976), pp. 54–57.

possible. What *is* relevant is that I awake from the dream in a cold sweat and remain troubled for the rest of the day; that my psyche is in a state of civil war, torn between what I want for myself and what my (introjected) father wants for me. To the extent that this dilemma remains unresolved, I shall be fragmented, un-whole; and since (Jung believed) the drive for wholeness is inherent in the psyche, my unconscious will send out dream after dream on this particular theme until I take steps to resolve the conflict. And because life is dialectical, so too will be my dream images. They will continue to violate the logical sequences of space and time, and to represent opposing concepts that, on closer examination, prove to be pretty much the same.

Jung's specific contribution, both to the history of alchemy and to depth psychology, was the discovery that patients with no previous knowledge of alchemy were having dreams that reproduced the imagery of alchemical texts with a bewildering similarity. In his famous essay, "Individual Dream Symbolism in Relation to Alchemy," Jung recorded a series of one such patient's dreams and produced for nearly every dream a separate alchemical plate that duplicated the dream symbols in an unmistakable way.[2] Inasmuch as Jung claimed that others had produced a similar set of dream images while

---

2 C.G. Jung, *The Collected Works of C. G. Jung*, vol. 14, trans. R.F.C. Hull, 2nd ed. (Princeton: Princeton University Press, 1961–1979), p. 12.

undergoing the individuation process, Jung was forced to conclude that this process was indeed inherent in the psyche and that the alchemists, without really knowing exactly what they were doing, had recorded the transformations of their own unconscious which they then projected onto the material world. The gold of which they spoke was thus not really gold, but a "golden" state of mind, the altered state of consciousness which overwhelms the person in an experience such as the Zen *satori* or the God-experience recorded by such Western mystics as Jakob Böhme (himself an alchemist), St. John of the Cross, or St. Teresa of Ávila. Far from being some pseudo-science or proto-chemistry, then, alchemy was fully real—the last major synthetic iconography of the human unconscious in the West. Or, in Norman O. Brown's terms, "the last effort of Western man to produce a science based on an erotic sense of reality."[3]

The rejection of alchemy as a science, in Jung's view, coincided with the repression of the unconscious characteristic of the West since the Scientific Revolution—a repression that he saw as having tragic consequences in the modern era, including widespread mental illness and orgies of genocide and barbarism.[4] Thus Jung believed that the failure of each individual to confront his own psychic demons, the part of his personality he

---

3 Norman O. Brown, *Life Against Death* (Middletown, CT: Wesleyan University Press, 1970), p. 316.

4 Of course, barbarism is hardly the prerogative of modern man, although its scale probably is. Jung would conceivably have argued that the creation of a

hated and feared (what Jung called the "shadow"), inevitably had disastrous consequences; and that the only hope, at least on the individual level, was to undertake the psychic journey that was in fact the essence of alchemy. In the cryptic words of the seventeenth-century alchemist and Rosicrucian, Michael Maier, "The sun and his shadow complete the work."[5] The creation of the self lies not in repressing the unconscious, but in reintroducing it to the conscious mind.[6]

---

technology necessary to effect the genocide of modern times was itself part of the process of psychic repression.

5 "*Sol et eius umbra perficiunt opus*," from a work of 1618, quoted by Dobbs in her study of Newton. B.J.T. Dobbs, *The Foundations of Newton's Alchemy* (Cambridge: Cambridge University Press, 1975), p. 31.

6 My description of Jung's work in this chapter is based on C.G. Jung, *The Collected Works of C.G. Jung*, vol. 14, trans. R.F.C. Hull, 2nd ed. (Princeton: Princeton University Press, 1961–1979), pp. 12, 14, 15; C.G. Jung, *Memories, Dreams, Reflections*, ed. Aniela Jaffe, trans. Richard and Clara Winston, rev. ed. (New York: Vintage Books, 1965); Anthony Storr, *Jung* (London: Fontana, 1973); Harold Stone, prologue to Dora M. Kalff, *Sandplay* (San Francisco: Browser Press, 1971); and B.J.T. Dobbs, *The Foundations of Newton's Alchemy* (Cambridge: Cambridge University Press, 1975), pp. 26–34.

Excerpted from Morris Berman, "The Disenchantment of the World (1)," in *The Reenchantment of the World* (Ithaca and New York: Cornell University Press, 1981), pp. 78–85.

Toward Individuation
C.G. Jung

The secret society is an intermediary stage on the way to individuation. The individual is still relying on a collective organization to effect his differentiation for him; that is, he has not yet recognized that it is really the individual's task to differentiate himself from all the others and stand on his own feet. All collective identities, such as membership in organizations, support of "isms," and so on, interfere with the fulfillment of this task. Such collective identities are crutches for the lame, shields for the timid, beds for the lazy, nurseries for the irresponsible; but they are equally shelters for the poor and weak, a home port for the shipwrecked, the bosom of a family for orphans, a land of promise for disillusioned vagrants and weary pilgrims, a herd and a safe fold for lost sheep, and a mother providing nourishment and growth. It would therefore be wrong to regard this intermediary stage as a trap; on the contrary, for a long time to come it will represent the only possible form of existence for the individual, who nowadays seems more than ever threatened by anonymity.

Nevertheless it may be that for sufficient reasons a man feels he must set out on his own feet along the road to wider realms. It may be that in all the garbs, shapes, forms, modes, and manners of life offered to him he does not find what is peculiarly necessary for him. He will go alone and be his own company. He will serve as his own group, consisting of a

TOWARD INDIVIDUATION

variety of opinions and tendencies—which need not necessarily be marching in the same direction. In fact, he will be at odds with himself, and will find great difficulty in uniting his own multiplicity for purposes of common action. Even if he is outwardly protected by the social forms of the intermediary stage, he will have no defense against his inner multiplicity. The disunion within himself may cause him to give up, to lapse into identity with his surroundings.

Like the initiate of a secret society who has broken free from the undifferentiated collectivity, the individual on his lonely path needs a secret which for various reasons he may not or cannot reveal. Such a secret reinforces him in the isolation of his individual aims. A great many individuals cannot bear this isolation. They are the neurotics, who necessarily play hide-and-seek with others as well as with themselves, without being able to take the game really seriously. As a rule they end by surrendering their individual goal to their craving for collective conformity—a procedure which all the opinions, beliefs, and ideals of their environment encourage. Only a secret which the individual cannot betray—one which he fears to give away, or which he cannot formulate in words, and which therefore seems to belong to the category of crazy ideas—can prevent the otherwise inevitable retrogression.

Adapted from C.G. Jung, "Late Thoughts," in *Memories, Dreams, Reflections*, trans. Richard and Clara Winston (New York: Vintage Books, 1989), pp. 342–344. First published in German in 1962.

Interview with Wolfgang Giegerich
Jonathan Simons

Many within the various schools of depth psychology consider Wolfgang Giegerich a controversial thinker. For over five decades, he has worked to redefine some of the most orthodox tenets of psychology, including its purpose, limitations, and relationship to both philosophy and empiricism. Giegerich sees most modern fields of psychology as blinded by technoscientific positivism and therefore ill-equipped to investigate matters of soul, dreams, interiority, and the human mind.

Born in the German city of Wiesbaden, Giegerich was awarded his PhD by the University of California, Berkeley and has since published more than two hundred essays and eighteen books. His collected papers in English encompass six volumes.[1] His work has made a significant impact on contemporary psychology worldwide, especially in Germany, the United States, the United Kingdom, Japan, Russia, and Brazil.

Dr. Giegerich has now retired from private practice and lives in Berlin, where he continues his research and writing. We were honored to meet him and discuss his theories, as well as his thoughts on our contemporary moment.

---

[1] Wolfgang Giegerich, *Collected English Papers*, vols. 1–6 (New Orleans: Spring Journal Books, 2005–2013).

INTERVIEW WITH WOLFGANG GIEGERICH

JONATHAN SIMONS: You've defined psychology as "the discipline of interiority." I imagine not every school of psychology—certainly not every psychologist—maintains that orientation. What's unique about depth psychology?

WOLFGANG GIEGERICH: Depth psychology is a generic term for all psychologies that work with a notion of the unconscious. But in my opinion, the only real depth psychology is Jungian psychology. Yet even most of Jung's work remains stuck on the notion of the person as the substrate of psychology. Whereas my idea of psychology as the discipline of interiority is concerned not with what goes on inside people but with a methodological approach to interiorizing phenomena into themselves. That means seeing these phenomena more deeply—seeing through to their essence. If psychology is the study of the *soul* (rather than the science of the *psyche* of the biological organism of humans), then its focus is the soul—the mercurial spirit—that animates the mind's objective products: its self-expression in dreams, symptoms, poems, works of art, religion, societal institutions, culture as a whole.

JS: Do you believe that intellectual thinking does not fully equip us to grasp what we might refer to as interiority or soul?

WG: Actually, we *are* equipped to do this, but we don't make use of the faculty. There have been branches of philosophy outlining tools for looking at things in this way, but modern psychology originated on a completely different footing; it was positivistic from the beginning. Whereas Jung, although he started out from the same groundwork, was interested in restoring some of the more traditional ways of looking at things.

Positivism arose after the collapse of metaphysics at the beginning of the nineteenth century, and it was a total break with the whole tradition—not only metaphysics, but also mythology, religion, and so on. Ultimately, positivism tries to eliminate, on principle, anything other than what can actually be demonstrated as empirical fact, and therefore it does not allow for any depth.

JS: In your book, *What Is Soul?*, you write, "Soul is the sense of the soul of and in the Real."[2] Can you elaborate on what you mean by *Real*?

WG: In this definition, I am not contrasting the Real with the unreal; rather, I am contrasting it with the traditional depth-psychological approach, which has to do with people's

---

2 Wolfgang Giegerich, *What Is Soul?* (New Orleans: Spring Journal, 2012), p. 26.

feelings, emotions, or fantasies and such. What I am trying to suggest is that there can still be an emphasis on "what is real outside of us"—on objective and cultural reality—and not just on subjective reality. In individuals, for example, symptoms are real; they are often very real, very terrible.

The words *fake* and *phony* and *simulation* are now prominent terms which illuminate much of our present reality and actually show a certain dialectic—namely, the fact that our present reality is becoming more and more a fake one.

JS: You've talked about the soul using the body for its own ends and purposes. Yet one of the central differences between your thinking and that of other Jungian scholars is that you don't see emotions as expressions of the soul. If not through thoughts or emotions, how does one discover the qualities and wishes of the soul?

WG: One important necessity is a developed feeling function, in Jung's sense of the term. If you have a developed feeling function, you can distinguish between great works of art and those that are not worth much. Or take wine-tasting or tea-tasting. There's this qualitative difference, something that you have to develop, and you can work at it, but there also has to be an aptitude for it. That's one thing.

Another thing you need is a concept of soul. And here I would like to introduce the idea that the soul is not actually a mysterious entity. "Soul" is simply the name I give to the invisible autonomous inner logic or mercurial spirit at work in real phenomena, in the transformations of the human mode of being in the world. Mythologically, the soul is connected to the underworld, to death—it's always logically negative (i.e., it is not empirical fact and also not ego). Practically, in therapy, one good means of access to soul is the symptom. That represents the ego-consciousness's other.

But in external reality, we can also distinguish between what, on the one hand, is relevant for the soul—for example, great works of art, literature, and philosophy—and, on the other, what is an ego product and interesting for the moment only—certain bestsellers, television programs, mere entertainment.

JS: It sounds almost as if you're saying that when you zoom out to the collective you're going to find soul, or the manifestations of soul. The extreme example would be that human beings were inevitably going to build an atomic bomb, and you've written about this. As hard as it is for one to swallow, you suggest that the atomic bomb is an expression of soul.

WG: Right, exactly. It's something real. The task of the psychologist would then be to see "the soul" in this reality. Modern humanity has the task of emancipating itself from the soul. The soul is not just something nice and beautiful and harmless. It can be terrible! Just like the Old Testament God—you had to both love *and* fear God. And if you keep this idea in mind, then I think you are not in danger of condoning or justifying certain human developments, like the atomic bomb.

JS: So soul is a force of nature.

WG: Yes. It is, as I said, the dynamic or logic invisibly at work in the historical changes in human relations to the world.

JS: If the task of psychology and analysis is to better understand soul, this implies that the process is not necessarily going to lead to one being a nicer, more beautiful, and compassionate person.

WG: Exactly. I think that has nothing to do with it. Psychology is not in the business of rescuing the world, of improving people. Maybe it's *improving* in the sense of making us see more, having a wider or deeper sense of reality, but there's nothing ethical about it. It's neutral.

JS: But let's say an individual is feeling that his or her life is meaningless and goes into analysis. Your way of understanding the reality of the soul is that there is no romanticized development in a specific direction towards beautification or towards compassion. So there's nothing to say that they won't find their life even more meaningless after analysis.

WG: Yes, the feeling of meaninglessness is not so rare. My colleagues in Japan have many young people who do not see the meaning of life. My reaction is, "Why do they need meaning?" I think the longing for meaning is a modern problem, a trap. It arose in the nineteenth century. Nobody talked about meaning before that, because meaning was clear: in life you had to be a good human being so that you were well placed in the afterlife.

JS: A lot of these existential problems are a product of modern individuation, whereas human history is mainly a history of collectivism. It doesn't surprise me that people coming from a society like Japan would now face these challenges, especially as American corporate media pushes them towards individuation.

WG: Right. This of course requires that you take this individuality seriously. Rather than listen to what other people tell you, find out what is really important for you and just be concerned with that. So many people are conditioned by their environment; they are not living out of themselves, to their own benefit. I think people have to discover who they are and find their own truth. That is all I'm trying to do: advocate that they see the world and themselves the way it is, and then make their choices.

I think what is to be sought is not a positive goal like "soul" or self-perfection, but rather a negative one: free yourself of illusions, and what is left is you. That's my approach in therapy.

JS: One of the reasons I appreciate that approach is precisely because it's not loaded with fallacies of positivity and happiness. I appreciate an idea common in many different Buddhist literatures and cultures, which is that to see truth is actually very difficult and painful. Being unhappy is not necessarily a sign of confusion, is it?

WG: No, not necessarily. I think truth often hurts. That's very clear. On the other hand, one doesn't have to dwell on subjects such as death, or old age, and things like that. We all know that we have to die, and that when we get old there will be hardships and illnesses, which isn't nice. You can choose to focus and dwell on death, but you don't have to.

JS: But it's hard to ignore it.

WG: I can only say personally that literal death doesn't mean anything to me. Just as I'm happy to go to bed at night, so I'll also be happy to die in old age. Of course, the moment of dying as a physiological, bodily act may be difficult, but it's perfectly normal. I think most people in the world have died so far [*laughs*]. So it's really nothing special.

JS: I'm thinking about Ernest Becker and *The Denial of Death*.³ His work suggests that culture is a product of our inability to accept the fact that we die; that's the impetus, he argues, for all human culture. So I wonder whether it's a rare occurrence to truly accept death without the support of religious myths. Were you always accepting of it? Or was that a process?

WG: I think always, yes. And concerning the theory of the denial of death as the impetus for culture, let me just remind you that for Plato philosophy is precisely the pursuit of death and dying. This is a psychological stance.

JS: What about longing? Longing for love and a meaningful life are quite universal. Is that because we humans have a soul?

WG: I wouldn't say we have a soul; rather, we *are* soul. Yes, I think that soul always has to do with the difference between what is here—immediate, at hand, practical and visible—and what is not here, not visible. "Negative," in that sense. And that tension can express itself in feelings of longing.

---

3   Ernest Becker, *The Denial of Death* (New York: Free Press, 1973).

JS: Would you say longing is yet another emotion, or is it a distinct phenomenon of the human being?

WG: It's very often an ego emotion. Emotions are always based on something physiological. But longing can also be something in its own right, a more logical relation to something—for example, an intellectual need for depth, or the soul's longing for the beyond.

JS: What interests me about longing is that it seems universal and timeless, whereas thoughts, fantasies, and possibly emotions, are culturally based. Even the infant, before it's conditioned, has longing. We could argue that it's just nature screaming for survival, but I wonder whether longing is a uniquely human phenomenon.

WG: I would think so, because I cannot imagine that animals long for anything. I think it's something specifically human and relates to the counter-natural form of existence of humans. We are not just body, physiology, and instinct—there is also this "more" that is not at hand.

JS: If we look objectively at human history, we see that the soul has its own development separate from our fantasies.

WG: Yes. It is autonomous. The soul has brought enormous changes in the course of history, and upheavals. For example, the French Revolution is a moment of soul; that is, an event that attests to a new logic of being in the world. Killing the king or sacrificial slaughter at the beginning of history — again that's "the soul's" need. It's not our human, our all-too-human interest. *We* don't want that.

JS: Your objective understanding gives you the insight into how the soul is and how it develops. I imagine that brings you a certain amount of peace and acceptance. At the same time, how do you, as a human being, feel about this world that we've created now?

WG: I'm very disappointed with certain sociopolitical developments. But I also think that in the long run — not during our lifetime — there is great potential if society manages to understand better what this is all about. It's really a cataclysmic change, and it needs a total reorientation, one for which we are not yet ready. What is going on now is pretty depressing, but it may not have to be if one finds different ways of dealing with it.

JS: My concern is that philosophical contemplation is becoming increasingly rare. Now it is the norm to be in states of distraction and hyperstimulation all of the time, and this produces a high level of fragmentation, which keeps a person on the surface of things. Under these conditions, where are the new philosophers and the next generation of poets going to come from?

WG: First of all, I think philosophers—the ones who really make a difference, the ones really capable of seeing what is happening in the world—have always numbered only very few individuals. So one shouldn't be too disturbed by the fact that the masses cannot do that.

The second point is that humans are humans, and there is an inner need in humanity to think, and you cannot quench that. So there will always remain a few individuals—and we don't need many—who have this need, who will not conform.

JS: After a life of thought, study, and psychological work, what do you have to say to younger people living in what we might call a new Dark Age, people who may feel both overwhelmed by the world yet also inspired by poetry and philosophy?

WG: I would say, first of all, that they have to resist feeling overwhelmed and follow their own need to love poetry and thinking. And secondly, they have to give up the illusion that they need to find like-minded others. They have to learn to be content with the loneliness of thought. They have to appreciate the thought itself and not be concerned about the result, the effect. I enjoy my thoughts. I'm not thinking of changing anything. I don't want to heal the world. I don't want to become famous or anything. No, I work quietly and publish some of my ideas, but whether or not people read them is their own business.

Jonathan Simons interviewed Wolfgang Giegerich in his home in Berlin on October 10, 2018.

Ikigai
Jeremy Page

To revere some god or other,
do good things, be kind;
to challenge the Absurd—
he gave all of these his best.

The question mark faded
from time to time
but proved indelible.

In despair
he excavated his past,
interrogated his future,
painted himself
in words and oils
to uncover who he was.

He learned
there was no god to revere
and the Absurd was unrelenting.
To do good things, be kind
was all that remained.

Ikigai (Japanese): a reason for being.

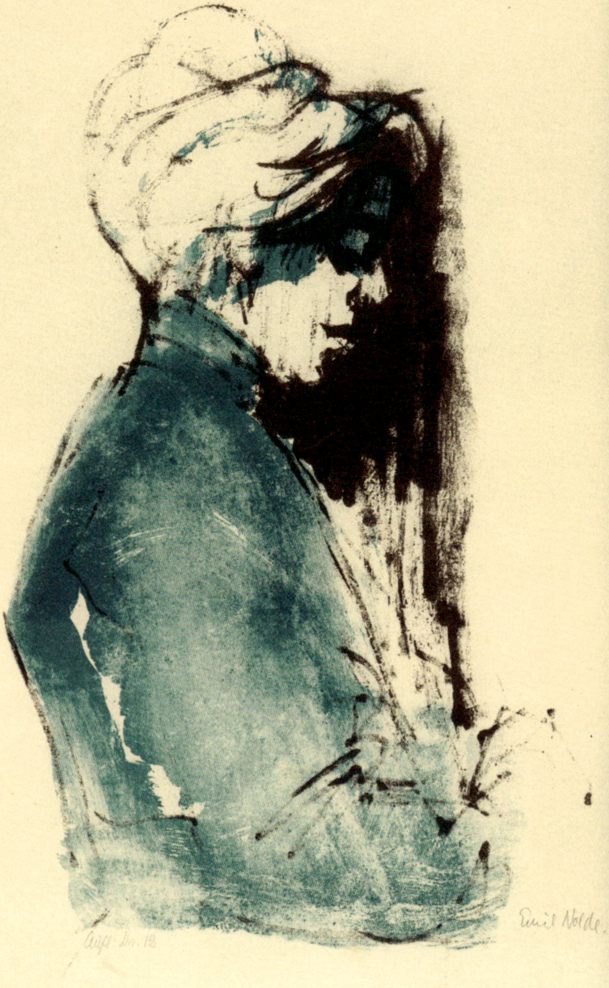
Emil Nolde.

Journal of a Solitude
May Sarton

Begin here. It is raining. I look out on the maple, where a few leaves have turned yellow, and listen to Punch, the parrot, talking to himself and to the rain ticking gently against the windows. I am here alone for the first time in weeks, to take up my "real" life again at last. That is what is strange—that friends, even passionate love, are not my real life unless there is time alone in which to explore and to discover what is happening or has happened. Without the interruptions, nourishing and maddening, this life would become arid. Yet I taste it fully only when I am alone here and "the house and I resume old conversations."[1]

On my desk, small pink roses. Strange how often the autumn roses look sad, fade quickly, frost-browned at the edges! But these are lovely, bright, singing pink. On the mantel, in the Japanese jar, two sprays of white lilies, recurved, maroon pollen on the stamens, and a branch of peony leaves turned a strange pinkish-brown. It is an elegant bouquet; *shibui*, the Japanese would call it. When I am alone the flowers are really seen; I can pay attention to them. They are felt as presences. Without them I would die. Why do I say that? Partly because they change before my eyes. They live and die

---

[1] May Sarton, "Der Abschied," in *Selected Poems of May Sarton* (Toronto: George J. McLeod Limited, 1978), p. 61.

in a few days; they keep me closely in touch with process, with growth, and also with dying. I am floated on their moments.

The ambience here is order and beauty. That is what frightens me when I am first alone again. I feel inadequate. I have made an open place, a place for meditation. What if I cannot find myself inside it?

I think of these pages as a way of doing that. For a long time now, every meeting with another human being has been a collision. I feel too much, sense too much, am exhausted by the reverberations after even the simplest conversation. But the deep collision is and has been with my unregenerate, tormenting, and tormented self. I have written every poem, every novel, for the same purpose—to find out what I think, to know where I stand. I am unable to become what I see. I feel like an inadequate machine, a machine that breaks down at crucial moments, grinds to a dreadful halt, "won't go," or, even worse, explodes in some innocent person's face.

Plant Dreaming Deep[2] has brought me many friends of the work (and also, harder to respond to, people who think they have found in me an intimate friend). But I have begun to realize that, without my own intention, that book gives a false view. The anguish of my life here—its rages—is hardly mentioned. Now I hope to break through into the rough

---

[2] May Sarton, *Plant Dreaming Deep* (New York: W.W. Norton & Company, Inc., 1968).

rocky depths, to the matrix itself. There is violence there and anger never resolved. I live alone, perhaps for no good reason, for the reason that I am an impossible creature, set apart by a temperament I have never learned to use as it could be used, thrown off by a word, a glance, a rainy day, or one drink too many. My need to be alone is balanced against my fear of what will happen when suddenly I enter the huge empty silence if I cannot find support there. I go up to Heaven and down to Hell in an hour, and keep alive only by imposing upon myself inexorable routines. I write too many letters and too few poems. It may be outwardly silent here but in the back of my mind is a clamor of human voices, too many needs, hopes, fears. I hardly ever sit still without being haunted by the "undone" and the "unsent." I often feel exhausted, but it is not my work that tires (work is a rest); it is the effort of pushing away the lives and needs of others before I can come to the work with any freshness and zest.

Excerpted from May Sarton, *Journal of a Solitude* (New York: W.W. Norton & Company, Inc., 1973), pp. 11–13.

What Is Difficult
Rainer Maria Rilke

And you should not let yourself be confused in your solitude by the fact that there is something in you that wants to move out of it. This very wish, if you use it calmly and prudently and like a tool, will help you spread out your solitude over a great distance. Most people have (with the help of conventions) turned their solutions toward what is easy and toward the easiest side of the easy; but it is clear that we must trust in what is difficult; everything alive trusts in it, everything in nature grows and defends itself any way it can and is spontaneously itself, tries to be itself at all costs and against all opposition. We know little, but that we must trust in what is difficult is a certainty that will never abandon us. It is good to be solitary, for solitude is difficult; that something is difficult must be one more reason for us to do it.

Excerpted from Rainer Maria Rilke, *Letters to a Young Poet*, trans. Stephen Mitchell (New York: Modern Library, 2001), pp. 67–68. First published in German as *Briefe an einen jungen Dichter* in 1929.

A Room at the Back
Patrick Curry

Solitude is best understood as a way of being in the world, what Ludwig Wittgenstein calls "a form of life."[1] It goes beyond shunning company—which is rarely possible to any great degree—to living in a way which places a high value, and sustained attention, on one's self.

And this is not necessarily egotistical if we accept that self and world are inseparable. We can distinguish between them, of course, but only ever in the sense that we perceive "inner" and "outer" as having different qualities. Both the self and the world are constituted by relationships; we are constantly making and being made through dances of mutual interdependency with other selves.

In his essay on solitude, Michel de Montaigne writes that it is not enough to withdraw from the multitude: "We have to withdraw from such attributes of the mob as are within us."[2] We must therefore take our soul back into our own possession.

The result of the self returning home to itself, he writes, "is true solitude." As such, it "can be enjoyed in towns and in kings' courts, but" (in a nicely laconic concession) "more

---

[1] Ludwig Wittgenstein, *Philosophical Investigations*, trans. Elizabeth Anscombe (Oxford: Blackwell, 2001), p. 75e. Wittgenstein himself loved solitude, but also feared it.

[2] Michel de Montaigne, *The Complete Essays*, trans. M.A. Screech (London: Penguin Books, 1991), p. 269.

conveniently apart."³ By the same token, partners, children, and goods are not a problem, precisely because the fulfillment which follows from "true solitude" doesn't completely depend on them — or, for that matter, on their absence.

How is one to carry through this idea of solitude as a way of life? Montaigne's famous advice is to "set aside a room, just for ourselves, at the back of the shop, keeping it entirely free and establishing there our true liberty, our principal solitude and asylum": *une arrière-boutique*, for one's self alone, behind the public self.⁴

I grant the importance of an indispensable minimum of sociality, which Montaigne tacitly admits when he counsels against seeking solitude by retreating to a deserted wilderness. But that does not mean that maintaining a private room at the back of one's shared life is not possible, desirable, or even necessary.

What about undue privilege? Doesn't Montaigne assume an elegant sufficiency of material goods and supplies? Indeed he does, and this point reminds us of the legitimate needs of the body and thence mind. It doesn't negate his advice, however. Given a sufficiency — not, note, an extravagance — it becomes possible, in principle, to develop a self with a high

---

3 Ibid.

4 Ibid., p. 270. See also M.A. Screech's excellent commentary in his *Montaigne and Melancholy: The Wisdom of the Essays* (Lanham: Rowland and Littlefield, 2000), pp. 67–70.

degree of integrity and durability, even though it is not invulnerable or eternal.

Relatedly, is his advice indefensibly quietistic? Isn't the personal political? Yes again, but it is not *only* political, and the history of the last century shows that when politics occupies and exhausts the personal, the result is barbarism of the worst sort: the Cultural Revolution, the Cambodian killing fields, Stalin's Great Terror.

Far from solitude being anti-social, or inducing passivity, some of its virtues are distinctly republican: self-awareness, and therefore recognition of others as equals; independence of thought and thence action; and courage, including the courage to stand alone if need be. Without enough individuals in the world who respect and embody these virtues, what hope remains of a relatively informed, responsible, and active citizenry? None, I would say.

Contemplation of the self throws into question the boundary between self and world; as Dōgen Zenji, the thirteenth-century Japanese Buddhist master wrote, "To study the self is to forget the self." And he goes on to say that "to forget the self is to be enlightened by everything."[5] We don't need to thank the pandemic for redirecting attention to our own selves and lives, nor lockdown for reminding us of

---

[5] Hakuun Yasutani, *Flowers Fall: A Commentary on Zen Master Dōgen's Genjōkōan* (Boston: Shambhala, 1996), p. 102.

solitude. Still less should we thank the virus for showcasing our appalling collective treatment of the natural world, including other animals, which was already crying out for rectification. Yet all this is no reason not to extract something positive, if we can.

THE TWENTY-FOURTH HEXAGRAM OF THAT ancient divinatory text the *I Ching*, or *Book of Changes*, is "Return." Richard Wilhelm's commentary on it particularly resonates with the spirit of Montaigne's work. He writes, "Things cannot be destroyed once and for all. When what is above is completely split apart, it returns below. Hence … *return* means coming back [and] leads to self-knowledge."[6] And during a time of return, "merchants and strangers [do] not go about, and the ruler [does] not travel through the provinces."[7] In other words, the ruler—whom we may take as any kind of sovereign—returns to where they properly live, and takes up residence once again in that room at the back.

This kind of return, it seems to me, is a good description of something we now urgently need to do. The resonance

---

6 *The I Ching or Book of Changes*, trans. Richard Wilhelm and Cary F. Baynes (Princeton: Princeton University Press, 1977), pp. 910–911. With a foreword by C.G. Jung. This translation of the Chinese classic text into English was first published in 1950 and was based on a translation into German, *I Ging. Das Buch der Wandlungen*, published in 1924.

7 Ibid., p. 258.

between Montaigne's humane and skeptical classical humanism and certain traditions of Chinese philosophy (historically and culturally completely unrelated) may not reveal a universal truth, but nor is it coincidence.[8]

What we have instead is something even more important: a *human* truth rooted in our relatively stable and enduring human nature, which is something not to be mastered but rather, like the rest of nature, to be respected and worked with. And in this context, the ruler who is being called upon to return home and refrain from touring the provinces, for now and until renewed, is the solitary self.

---

8 That is particularly true of neo-Confucianism, running from the eleventh to the fifteenth centuries, with its emphasis on developing and maintaining a unique self through careful and responsible sociality. Arguably its most important philosopher, Zhi Xi (1130–1200), was also the *I Ching*'s most influential commentator. See, for example, William Theodore de Bary, *Learning for Oneself: Essays on the Individual in Neo-Confucian Thought* (New York: Columbia University Press, 1991).

Adapted from an essay handwritten by the author in an Analog Sea *Notes on Solitude* notebook.

The Man in His Tower
Kenneth Clark

What could an intelligent, open-minded man do in mid-sixteenth-century Europe? Keep quiet, work in solitude, outwardly conform, inwardly remain free. The wars of religion evoked a figure new to European civilization, although familiar in the great ages of China: the intellectual recluse. Petrarch and Erasmus had used their brains at the highest level of politics. They had been the advisers of princes. Their successor, the greatest humanist of the mid sixteenth century, retreated into his tower (a real tower, not the "ivory tower" of cliché language). This was Michel de Montaigne. He was a fairly conscientious mayor of Bordeaux, but he refused to go any nearer to the center of power. He had no illusions about the effect of the religious convictions released by the Reformation. "In trying to make themselves angels," he said, "men transform themselves into beasts."

He was born in southern France in 1533. His mother was a Jewish Protestant, his father a Catholic who achieved wide culture as well as a considerable fortune. But not only was Montaigne detached from the two religious factions, he was completely skeptical about the Christian religion altogether. He said, "I would willingly carry a candle in one hand for St Michael and a candle for his Dragon in the other." His essays are as crammed with quotations as are the tracts of the warring priests, but instead of being texts from the Bible they are quotations from the authors of Greece and Rome, whose works he seems to have known almost by heart. But far more important than this classical learning was his unequaled detachment. Only two emotions had stirred his heart, his love of his father, and his friendship, like that of Tennyson for Hallam, for a man named La Boétie;[1] and when they had both died, he retired into himself. Only one thing engaged his mind—to tell the truth. But it was a concept of truth very different from that which serious men had sought in Colet's sermons or Erasmus's New Testament. It involved always looking at the other side of every question, however shocking, by conventional standards, that other side might be. And it was a truth that depended on the testimony of the only person he could examine without shame or scruple: himself. In the past, self-examination had been painful and penitential. To Montaigne it was a pleasure, and as he says, "No pleasure hath any savor unless I can communicate it." In order to do so he invented the essay, which was to remain the accepted form of humanist communication for three centuries, from Bacon to Hazlitt.

These self-searchings really mark the end of the heroic spirit of the Renaissance. As Montaigne says, "Sit we upon the highest throne in the world, yet sit we only upon our own tail."

---

[1] Étienne de La Boétie (1530–1563) was a French judge, poet, and close friend of Montaigne. —*Analog Sea Editor*

The strange thing is that people on high thrones didn't resent Montaigne: on the contrary, they sought his company. Had he lived, his friend Henry IV might have forced him to become Chancellor of France. But he preferred to remain in his tower.

Excerpted from Kenneth Clark, "Protest and Communication," in *Civilisation* (London: BBC and John Murray, 1969), pp. 161–163. Michel de Montaigne's *Essais* were first published in Middle French in 1580.

Remaining Oneself
Stefan Zweig

It is crucial then that we strive to understand the art of living, the wise way of living according to Montaigne, and to realize that this struggle leads to the discovery of *soi-même*,[1] the most crucial struggle of the spirit, exemplified by his own life. We too need to stand the test, to endure one of the most horrifying collapses of humanity, which follows directly one of its most magnificent periods of advancement. We too are to be torn from our hopes, from our experiences, our expectations and our enthusiasms, chased out from them as if under the whip, until we have only our naked self left to defend, that unique being which is irreplaceable. It was only when destiny made us brothers that Montaigne granted me his aid, his consolation, his irreplaceable friendship; how his fate indeed seems so very similar to our own! When Michel de Montaigne made his entry into the world, a great hope was beginning to die, the same hope that we experienced at the opening of our century: that of a more humanistic world. In the space of a single generation, the Renaissance had lavished on humanity a gift that enabled its artists, painters, thinkers, its seers and poets to reach a level of perfection none had anticipated. A century—no, centuries—were opening up where creative power, step by step, wave on wave, was

---

1 Oneself.

carrying dark and chaotic existence towards the threshold of the divine. All at once the world had become vaster, richer. With Greek and Latin, the scholars rediscovered antiquity and gave back to mankind the wisdom of Plato and Aristotle. Under the guidance of Erasmus, humanism promised a unified and cosmopolitan culture; the Reformation seemed, alongside the new scope of knowledge, to have founded a new religious freedom. Distances, borders between peoples, were beginning to dissolve, for printing, which had just been invented, gave to each word, to each thought, the means to soar, to spread; that which had once been the reserve of a single people seemed now open to all; a spirit of unity was emerging beyond the bloody quarrels of kings, princes, and armies. And another miracle: just like the spiritual world, the terrestrial world was expanding in dimensions no one could have conceived. Across an ocean thought impassable emerged new shores, new countries, a great uncharted continent, promising a safe haven for future generations. The arteries of commerce experienced ever livelier pulsations, a wave of riches extended across old Europe leaving luxury in its wake, and in its turn the luxury left buildings, paintings, statues—a highly decorated, spiritualized world. And always when there is more space, the soul opens up. So it was at the beginning of our own century, when, once more, space increased in grandiose fashion thanks to the conquest of the ether by flight, thanks to physics, chemistry, technology. As science drew from nature her secrets one after another and revealed those secrets in the service of man, an inexpressible hope animated a humanity so often disappointed, and from a million souls arose Ulrich von Hutten's jubilant cry: "What joy it is to live!"

But always when the wave climbs too high and too quickly, it falls the more violently, like a cataract. And just as, in our time, the miracles of technology have morphed into the most horrific elements of destruction, so elements of the Renaissance and humanism which at first seemed to offer salvation proved a lethal poison. The Reformation, which dreamt of bringing to Europe a new Christian spirit, provoked unrestrained barbarism in the wars of religion; the printing press did not diffuse culture but *furor theologicus*;[2] instead of humanism it was intolerance that spread. Across the whole of Europe, a murderous civil war devastated each country, while in the new world the bestial excesses of the conquistadors led to unparalleled cruelty. The century of Raphael and Michelangelo, of Dürer and Erasmus, permitted the atrocities of Attila, Genghis Khan, and Tamerlane.

How, in spite of its infallible clear-sightedness, in spite of the pity set deep in its soul, was humanity obliged to suffer this terrifying descent into bestiality, through one of those sporadic outbursts of insanity which sometimes seize it, just like that which we endure today? In this question lies the

---

2 Theological protest.

real tragedy of Montaigne. At no moment in his life did he see reign in his country, or the world at large, peace, reason, or tolerance, all those higher spiritual forces to which he had devoted his inner calling. When he opens his eyes to look out on the world and then lowers his gaze, he turns aside, like us stricken with horror at this mob frenzy of fury and hate which debilitates and profanes his homeland and humanity. He is still virtually a child, no more than fifteen years old, when, before his eyes, the riots against the *gabelle*[3] are ferociously repressed in Bordeaux, exhibiting an inhumanity which will leave him for the rest of his days the sworn enemy of all cruelty.

In such epochs where the highest values of life—our peace, our independence, our basic rights, all that makes our existence more pure, more beautiful, all that justifies it—are sacrificed to the demon inhabiting a dozen fanatics and ideologues, all the problems of the man who fears for his humanity come down to the same question: how to remain free? How to preserve the incorruptible lucidity of my spirit faced with all the threats and dangers of sectarian turmoil? How to keep humanity intact in the throes of bestiality? How to escape the tyrannical demands that the state and Church seek to impose on me? How to protect that unique part of my soul against enforced submission to rules and measures dictated from outside? How to safeguard the deepest region of my spirit and its

---

3 A tax on salt.

matter which belongs to me alone, my body, my health, my thoughts, my feelings, from the danger of being sacrificed to the deranged prejudices of others, to serve interests which are not my own?

It is to this question and this question alone that Montaigne dedicated his life and his strength. It is for this love of liberty that he observes himself, watches over, experiences and criticizes every movement and every sensation. And this quest, which he undertakes to safeguard his soul, his liberty, at a moment of universal servility before ideologies and parties, makes him today a brother to us, more intimate than any other artist. If we love and honor him today more than any other, it is because he devoted himself more than any other to the most sublime art of living: *rester soi-même*.[4]

---

4 To remain oneself.

Adapted from Stefan Zweig, *Montaigne*, trans. Will Stone (London: Pushkin Press, 2015), pp. 40–48. First published in German in 1942.

That Stroke of the Lighthouse
Virginia Woolf

For now she need not think about anybody. She could be herself, by herself. And that was what now she often felt the need of—to think; well not even to think. To be silent; to be alone. All the being and the doing, expansive, glittering, vocal, evaporated; and one shrunk, with a sense of solemnity, to being oneself, a wedge-shaped core of darkness, something invisible to others. Although she continued to knit, and sat upright, it was thus that she felt herself; and this self having shed its attachments was free for the strangest adventures. When life sank down for a moment, the range of experience seemed limitless. And to everybody there was always this sense of unlimited resources, she supposed; one after another, [we] must feel, our apparitions, the things you know us by, are simply childish. Beneath it is all dark, it is all spreading, it is unfathomably deep; but now and again we rise to the surface and that is what you see us by. Her horizon seemed to her limitless. There were all the places she had not seen; the Indian plains; she felt herself pushing aside the thick leather curtain of a church in Rome. This core of darkness could go anywhere, for no one saw it. They could not stop it, she thought, exulting. There was freedom, there was peace, there was, most welcome of all, a summoning together, a resting on a platform of stability. Not as oneself did one find rest ever, in her experience (she accomplished here something dexterous with her needles), but as a wedge of darkness. Losing personality, one lost the fret, the hurry, the stir; and there rose to her lips always some exclamation of triumph over life when things came together in this peace, this rest, this eternity; and pausing there she looked out to meet that stroke of the Lighthouse, the long steady stroke, the last of the three, which was her stroke, for watching them in this mood always at this hour one could not help attaching oneself to one thing especially of the things one saw; and this thing, the long steady stroke, was her stroke. Often she found herself sitting and looking, sitting and looking, with her work in her hands until she became the thing she looked at—that light for example. […]

It was odd, she thought, how if one was alone, one leant to things, inanimate things; trees, streams, flowers; felt they expressed one; felt they became one; felt they knew one, in a sense were one; felt an irrational tenderness thus (she looked at that long steady light) as for oneself. There rose, and she looked and looked with her needles suspended, there curled up off the floor of the mind, rose from the lake of one's being, a mist, a bride to meet her lover.

Excerpted from Virginia Woolf, *To the Lighthouse* (London: J.M. Dent & Sons Ltd, 1963), pp. 72–74. First published in 1927.

Letters from Shenandoah
Jean James

From the hedge of her mind
she sends letters back to the island.

They say
that here nothing is fixed
that life climbs up from the roots
that nothing is separate
that you can tell a wood by chewing it
that days stretch out kite-tailed
that this country rolls on back and back,
quilted in blue grass and fractured greenstone.

She talks of how a woman
can feel lost here
looking,
that bushes are wired with swallowtails
that Queen Anne's Lace mantles the fields
that fruit cellars groan with apples
that the mare is fetlocked in moonlight
that pine and oak and chestnut
proffer their limbs for homes and barns.

After dusk she sits
in the oil lamp's circle

with Joseph in the corner asleep
mumbling something about judgement,
and she feels the house moving within them
in the powder of earth after rain.

Later,
settling her head on the flanks of night,
she can see the shadow
of her empty dress, still warm,
its rose sleeves outflung on the back of the chair
waiting to surprise her again.

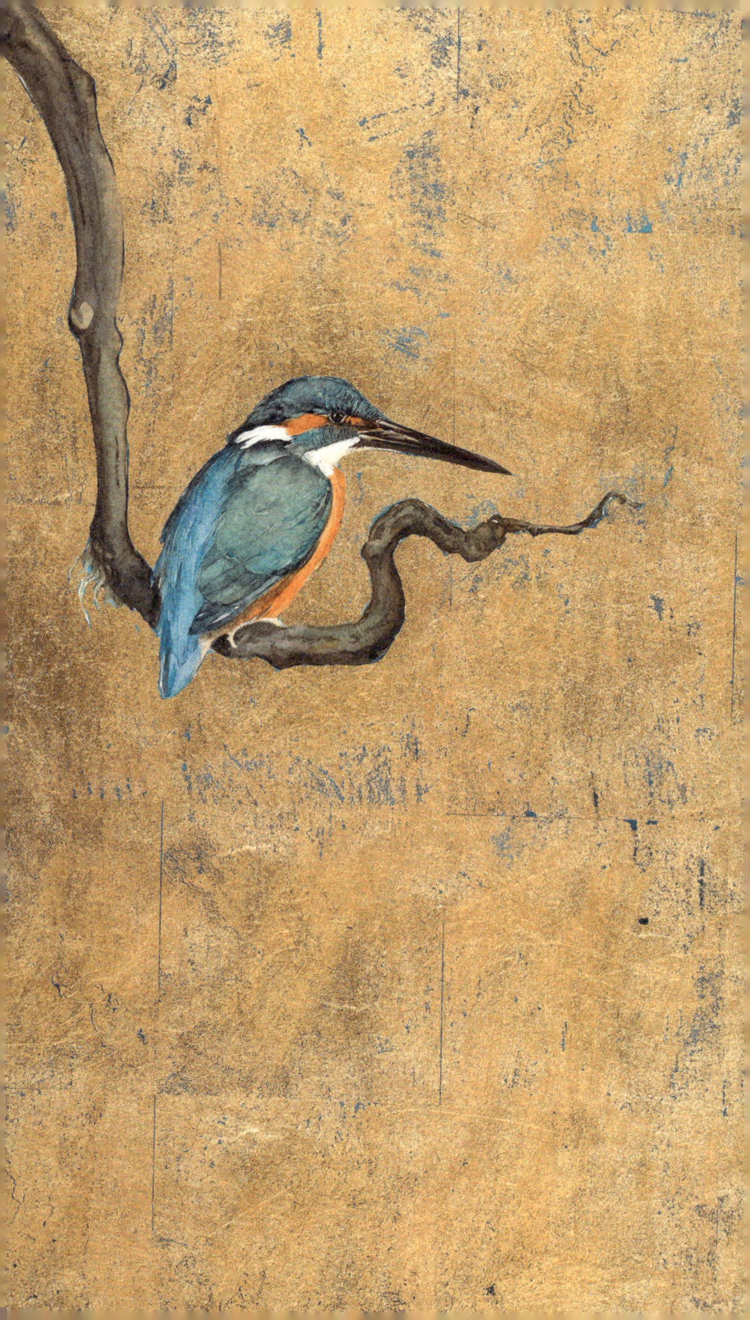

Silt
Robert Macfarlane

Half a mile offshore, walking on silver water, we found a curved path that extended gracefully and without apparent end to our north and south. It was a shallow tidal channel and the water it held caught and pooled the sun, such that its route existed principally as flux; a phenomenon of light and of currents. Its bright line curved away from us: an ogee or line of beauty whose origin we could not explain and whose invitation to follow we could not disobey, so we walked it northwards, along that glowing track made neither of water nor of land, which led us further and still further out to sea.

Out and on we walked, barefoot over and into the mirror-world. I glanced back at the coast. The air was grainy and flickering, like an old newsreel. The sea wall had hazed out to a thin black strip. Structures of unknown purpose—a white-beamed gantry, a low-slung barracks—showed on the shoreline. Every few hundred yards, I dropped a white cockleshell. The light had modified again, from nacreous to granular to dense. Sound traveled oddly. The muted pop-popping of gunfire was smudgy, but the call of a cuckoo from somewhere on the treeless shore rang sharply to us. A pale sun glared through the mist, its white eye multiplying in pools and ripples.

With so few orientation points and so many beckoning paths, we were finding it hard to stay on course. I was experiencing a powerful desire to walk straight out to sea and explore the greater freedoms of this empty tidal world. But we were both still anxious about straying far from the notional path of the Broomway and encountering the black muds or the quicksands.

My thoughts were beginning to move unusually, worked upon and changed by the mind-altering surfaces of this offshore world and by the elation that arose from walking securely on water. Out there, nothing could be only itself. The eye's vision fed on false color values. Similes, metaphors, and illusions bred. Ideas of opposition felt outflanked, melted away. Gull-eagles dipped and glided in the outer reaches of the mist. The sand served as the water's tain: "tain," from the French for "tin," being the lusterless backing of a mirror which makes reflection possible but limits the onward gaze, disallowing the view of a concept or idea beyond that point.

Walking always with us were our reflections, our attentive ghost selves. For the water acted as a mirror line, such that we both appeared joined at the ankles with our doubles, me more than twelve feet tall and David a foot taller still. If anyone had been able to look out from the shore, through the mist, they would have seen two giant walkers striding over the sea.

Several years ago the sculptor Antony Gormley buried a full-size iron cast of his own body upside down in the ground of Cambridge's Archaeological Research Institute. Only the undersides of the iron man's feet show on the surface. Two days before coming to walk the Broomway I had slipped off my shoes and socks and stood barefoot in the rusty prints, sole to sole with that buried body. Now that act of doubling had itself been unexpectedly repeated out here on the sands. Everywhere I looked were pivot points and fulcrums, symmetries and proliferations: the thorax points of a winged world. Sand mimicked water, water mimicked sand, and the air duplicated the textures of both. Hinged cuckoo calls; razor shells and cockleshells; our own reflections; a profusion of suns; the glide of transparent over solid. When I think back to the outer miles of that walk, I now recall a strong disorder of perception that caused illusions of the spirit as well as of the eye. I recall thought becoming sensational; the substance of landscape so influencing mind that mind's own substance was altered.

Felt pressure, sensed texture, and perceived space can work upon the body and so too upon the mind, altering the textures and inclinations of thought. The American farmer and writer Wendell Berry suggests this in a fine essay called "The Rise," in which he describes setting float in a canoe on a river in spate. "No matter how deliberately we moved from the shore into the sudden violence of a river on the rise," writes Berry, "there would ... be several uneasy minutes of transition. The river is another world, which means that one's senses and reflexes must begin to live another life."

We lack — we need — a term for those places where one experiences a "transition" from a known landscape into "another world": somewhere we feel and think differently. I have for some time now been imagining such transitions as border crossings. These borders do not correspond to national boundaries, and papers and documents are unrequired at them. Their traverse is generally unbiddable, and no reliable map exists of their routes and lines. They exist even in familiar landscapes: there when you cross a certain watershed, mountain pass, treeline, or snowline, or enter rain, storm, or mist, or pass from boulder clay onto sand, or chalk onto greenstone. Such moments are rites of passage that reconfigure local geographies, leaving known places suddenly outlandish or quickened, revealing continents within countries.

What might we call such incidents and instances—or, rather, how to name the lands that are found beyond these frontiers? "Xenotopias," perhaps, meaning "foreign places" or "out-of-place places," a term to complement our utopias and our dystopias. Martin Martin, the traveler and writer who in the 1690s set sail to explore the Scottish seaboard, knew that one does not need to displace oneself vastly within space to find difference. "It is a piece of weakness and folly merely to value things because of their distance from the place where we are born," he wrote in 1697, "thus men have traveled far enough in the search of foreign plants and animals, and yet continue strangers to those produced in their own natural climate." So did Henry David Thoreau: "An absolutely new prospect is a great happiness, and I can still get this any afternoon. Two or three hours' walking will carry me to as strange a country as I expect ever to see. A single farmhouse which I had not seen before is sometimes as good as the dominions of the King of Dahomey."

The American writer William Fox has spent his career exploring what he calls "cognitive dissonance in isotropic spaces," which might be more plainly translated as "how we get easily lost in spaces that appear much the same in all directions." Fox's thesis is that we are unable to orient ourselves in self-similar landscapes because we evolved in the dense, close-hand environments of jungle and savannah. In repetitive, data-depleted landscapes with few sight markers "our natural navigation abilities begin to fail catastrophically." Fox visited the Antarctic, the American deserts, and volcanic calderas in the Pacific to explore such monotone spaces—but David and I had stumbled into one a few hundred yards off the Essex coast.

The serenity of the space through which we were moving calmed me to the point of invulnerability, and thus we walked on. A mile out, the white mist still hovered, and in the haze I started to perceive impossible forms and shapes: a fleet of Viking longboats with high lug-rigged square sails; a squadron of feluccas, dhows, and *sgoths*; cityscapes (the skyline of Istanbul, the profile of the Houses of Parliament). When I looked back, the coastline was all but imperceptible, and it was apparent that our footprints had been erased behind us, and so we splashed tracelessly on out to the tidal limit. It felt at that moment wholly true that a horizon might exert as potent a pull upon the mind as a mountain's summit.

Eventually, reluctantly, nearly two miles offshore, with the tide approaching its turn and our worries at last starting to rise through our calm—black mud through sand—we began a long slow arc back towards the coastline and the path of the Broomway, away from the outermost point. There was the return of bearings, the approach to land, a settling to recognizability. As we returned to shore, we laid plans to walk the Broomway again, later in the year, but this time at night.

Mud-caked and silly with the sun and the miles, a pair of Mesolithic tramps, we left the sand where it met the causeway near Wakering Stairs. There at the causeway's frayed end, on the brink of the Black Grounds, were the marker poles, and—perched on the top of their stand of eelgrass—were my faithful trainers. I put them on and we walked out of Doggerland, or whichever country it was that we had discovered that day, off the mirror and onto the sea wall. For days afterwards I felt calm, level, shining, sand-flat.

Adapted from Robert Macfarlane, "Silt" in *The Old Ways: A Journey on Foot* (London: Penguin Books, 2013), pp. 57–81.

Spinning Stories
David Abram

But what, then, of writing? It would be a perilous mistake for any reader to conclude that he or she should simply relinquish the written word. Indeed, the written word carries a pivotal magic—the same magic that once sparkled for us in the eyes of an owl and the glide of an otter.

For those of us who care for an earth not encompassed by machines, a world of textures, tastes, and sounds other than those that we have engineered, there can be no question of simply abandoning literacy, of turning away from all writing. Our task, rather, is that of *taking up* the written word, with all of its potency, and patiently, carefully, writing language back into the land. Our craft is that of releasing the budded, earthly intelligence of our words, freeing them to respond to the speech of the things themselves—to the green uttering-forth of leaves from the spring branches. It is the practice of spinning stories that have the rhythm and lilt of the local soundscape, tales for the tongue, tales that want to be told, again and again, sliding off the digital screen and slipping off the lettered page to inhabit these coastal forests, those desert canyons, those whispering grasslands and valleys and swamps. Finding phrases that place us in contact with the trembling neck-muscles of a deer holding its antlers high as it swims toward the mainland, or with the ant dragging a scavenged rice-grain through the grasses. Planting words, like seeds, under rocks and fallen logs—letting language take root, once again, in the earthen silence of shadow and bone and leaf.

AN ALDER LEAF, LOOSENED BY wind, is drifting out with the tide. As it drifts, it bumps into the slender leg of a great blue heron staring intently through the rippled surface, then drifts on. The heron raises one leg out of the water and replaces it, a single step. As I watch, I, too, am drawn into the spread of silence. Slowly, a bank of cloud approaches, slipping its bulged and billowing texture over the earth, folding the heron and the alder trees and my gazing body into the depths of a vast breathing being, enfolding us all within a common flesh, a common story now bursting with rain.

Adapted from David Abram, *The Spell of the Sensuous* (New York: Vintage Books, 1996), pp. 273–274.

In Search of Darkness
Maria Browning

I don't remember ever being afraid of the dark. If my mother were still alive perhaps she'd remind me of times when I begged to leave the light on at bedtime or came scurrying into my parents' room, terrified of monsters that lurked in the pitch-black corners of my own.

But what *I* remember is standing on the back seat of a Galaxie 500, looking out the rear window as my mother drives along unlit country roads. I stare, with a deep thrill I can't name, at the black sky above and then at the rushing road below, so briefly illuminated by the car's taillights before it disappears into endless shadow.

I remember breathing in the cold of a moonless winter night as I stand, alone, on a hillside near our house. The lights of home are somewhere behind me, but in front of me there's nothing but a darkness so profound I can't be sure where the sky meets the earth. Joy stirs in me and then falls away as I become lost to myself, one with everything.

I remember wandering in the woods as evening falls, the shadows growing and deepening between the trees, night filling up the world. There's a power carried on this darkness — primal, living magic. I can feel it enter me. Anything is possible.

I remember lying in bed in the windowless attic of my grandmother's house, shut away from the lighted rooms below, from the streetlights outside. I feel weightless and free.

In all these memories I am alone, or effectively alone. Even in the car, I am alone with my thoughts, my mother silent and absorbed in thoughts of her own. The deep beauty of darkness can emerge only in solitude, it seems.

I can recollect plenty of other long-ago experiences in the dark—nights camping on a remote lakeside with my family, ghost stories around campfires and sleepover flashlight games with gaggles of shrieking girls. There was no magic in any of that.

All these memories are from my rural childhood fifty years ago, when darkness was much more abundant, when it took over the world each night and artificial lights were so scarce they barely registered in the black expanse.

We've mostly lost the darkness now. Even deep in the country, half the houses are adorned with glaring twenty-four-hour lights that push into the surrounding woods and invade the sky. In more urban places there's scarcely a dark corner left. The whole world is lit up like an interstate truck stop, nominally to make us safer.

Perhaps it does, to a degree, though the apparent belief that security is directly proportional to lumens seems pretty dubious. And we still don't seem to *feel* any safer. Does all that unnatural light help us look one another in the eye more readily, trust our neighbors more, greet the strangers we can see so clearly? Not that I can tell.

IN SEARCH OF DARKNESS

When I bought my house in this small town outside Nashville more than twenty years ago, there was not a streetlight visible in any direction, and everyone along the road turned off the outdoor lights at bedtime. On a moonless night, the darkness was broken only by the headlights of passing cars. I used to step outside my door on summer nights just to stare at the Milky Way. I wish I had done it more. As the lights of development have crept in, the Milky Way has faded, receding like a delicate plant under a brutal sun.

Now I step outside my door and stare at the bank of round-the-clock lights from the new houses that have been built on a nearby hillside—potent blue LED lights that assault the eye, even from a hundred yards away. I try hard to make peace with the presence of those lights, to see them as cozy reminders of human presence, as *neighbors*, with all the warm associations that can, at least potentially, entail.

This never works.

Instead, I find myself looking at them compulsively, helplessly, with mild horror—as you might stare at a rash spreading up your arm. The only alternative is to look deliberately away, which is not a comfort. I can't pretend the lights aren't there. I'm not blessed with a gift for ignoring problems.

And I can't help seeing it as a problem. I crave the night so much, miss it *so much*. This feeling grows in me with every year that passes, and not only because the lights have become increasingly hard to escape. Something in me is changing, and it's not just the lights that have become intolerable but the driven, narcissistic mode of life they accompany.

Something deep within me recoils from it all and longs to turn toward darkness. Night is when the body goes to ground and the soul comes forth. I knew that as a child, forgot for a while, and now, with age, the knowledge is coming back, forcing itself into my awareness every time I see that bank of lights.

I'm not alone in this, I'm sure. My mother, as she entered old age, sold her house and moved out into the woods, to a place where revved-up, lit-up modern life barely intruded at all—no sound of traffic, the night unmarred by lights of any kind.

She had a lot of reasons for putting herself so far from the nominal safety of the well-lit world, but the one she always fell back on, the one none of us could argue against, was that she felt at peace there. "I can be in nature," she said, and I understand now that she meant more by that than listening to birdsong and watching the leaves turn in the fall. She could *be* in a way that felt impossible elsewhere. She could go to ground and let her soul come forth.

My mother died a few months ago. I wish I could say she spent her last days in that peaceful refuge she'd found, but in fact dementia robbed her of it. Unreasoning fear took away the consolation she found in unbroken night. She spent the last year of her life in the locked ward of a nursing home, where the lights stayed on twenty-four hours a day. She simply dropped dead there one morning, and it's hard not to see that as a deliverance.

Since then I've spent a lot of time alone in her house in the woods, going through her things, sorting the relics and debris of her life. I've been there as darkness falls, a darkness deeper than any I normally see anywhere now. It surrounds and draws me in, and I am taken back to that young self who knew how to surrender to it, to be liberated by it. I'm learning again how to *be in nature*, my true nature. Deliverance beckons. Slowly, inexorably, I'm following my mother into the dark.

Newgrange
Thomas R. Smith

The guide recommends that claustrophobes enter last, should the narrow, enclosed passage prove too intense. Cautiously, I hang toward the back as we file, about twenty of us, into the low doorway of this strangely contemporary-looking dome-like structure we glimpsed on its far green hill while approaching.

Crossing the slab threshold, edging sideways to squeeze between the massive wall rocks, I feel the numbers become physical—five thousand years old, two hundred eighty feet in diameter, two hundred thousand tons of rock and earth. My discomfort slowly gives way to admiration and then to keen curiosity about the neolithic society capable of realizing such a monumental feat of engineering, a millennium before the Great Pyramid of Giza.

Sixty feet in, we crowd the inner sanctum, an uneasy roominess opening beneath the corbeled ceiling. I can't decide whether this weight I sense around and above me is of stone or time.

We know that cremated remains were brought here. Possibly the flint-hewn basins were for birthing. On sunrise at Winter Solstice light plays down the passage all the way to the inner chamber for about seventeen minutes, assuming clear weather, which in Ireland one can't. We imagine the shortest day arriving for those mysterious dwellers along the Boyne, the name by which they knew the river, a part of that unraveled fabric of their lives.

The guide informs us he's switching off his lamp. Ancient darkness rushes in. We are blind in the earth. Now, slowly, electric light grows from the "roofbox" window over the entrance, lays down a ragged path, heavily shadowing the spiral incisions on walls. I hear myself letting out held breath as the weakly cheerful artificial sun relieves the tomb-darkness. It's as if a prayer has laid its light over some intractable fact of living, this pathway one of those channels prayer has carved in the human heart over thousands of years, laying luminous hands on the stones of the world.

To Live Wisely
Barry Lopez

The individual's dream, whether it be so private a wish as that the joyful determination of nesting arctic birds might infuse a distant friend weary of life, or a magnanimous wish, that a piece of scientific information wrested from the landscape might serve one's community—in individual dreams is the hope that one's own life will not have been lived for nothing. The very much larger dream, that of a people, is a story we have been carrying with us for millennia. It is a narrative of determination and hope that follows a question: what will we do as the wisdom of our past bears down on our future? It is a story of ageless conversation, not only conversation among ourselves about what we mean and wish to do, but a conversation held with the land—our contemplation and wonder at a prairie thunderstorm, or before the jagged line of a young mountain, or at the sudden rise of ducks from an isolated lake. We have been telling ourselves the story of what *we* represent in the land for forty thousand years. At the heart of this story, I think, is a simple, abiding belief: it is possible to live wisely on the land, and to live well. And in behaving respectfully toward all that the land contains, it is possible to imagine a stifling ignorance falling away from us.

Excerpted from Barry Lopez, preface to *Arctic Dreams* (London: Vintage Classics, 2014), p. xxxiv. First published in 1986.

Every Morning All Over Again
William Stafford

Only the world guides me.
Weather pushes, or when it entices
I follow. Some kind of magnetism
turns me when I am walking
in the woods with no intentions.

There are leadings without any
reason, but they attract;
if I find there is nothing to gain
from them, I still follow — their power
is the power of the surrounding world.

But things that promise, or those
that will serve my purposes — they
interfere with the pure wind
from nowhere that sustains a kite,
or a gull, or a free spirit.

So, afloat again every morning,
I find the current: all the best
rivers have secret channels that
you have to find by whispering
like this, and then hear them and follow.

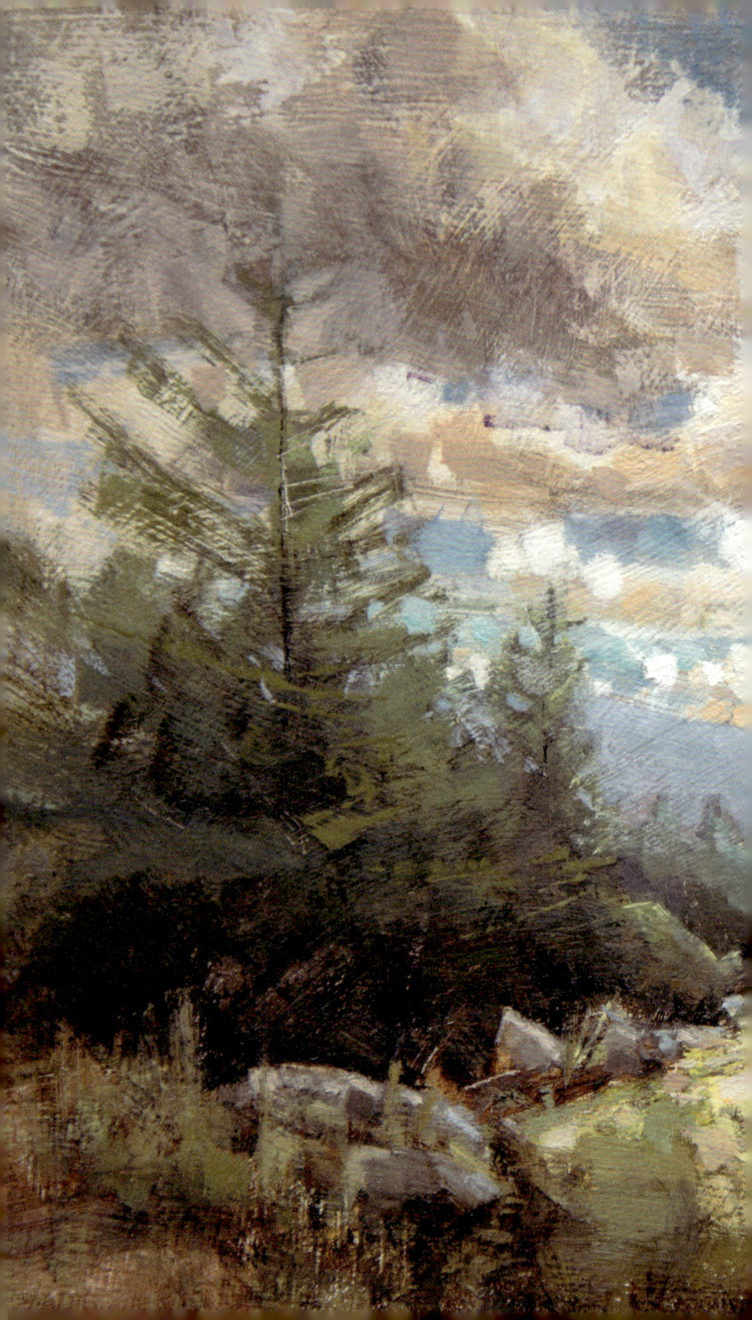

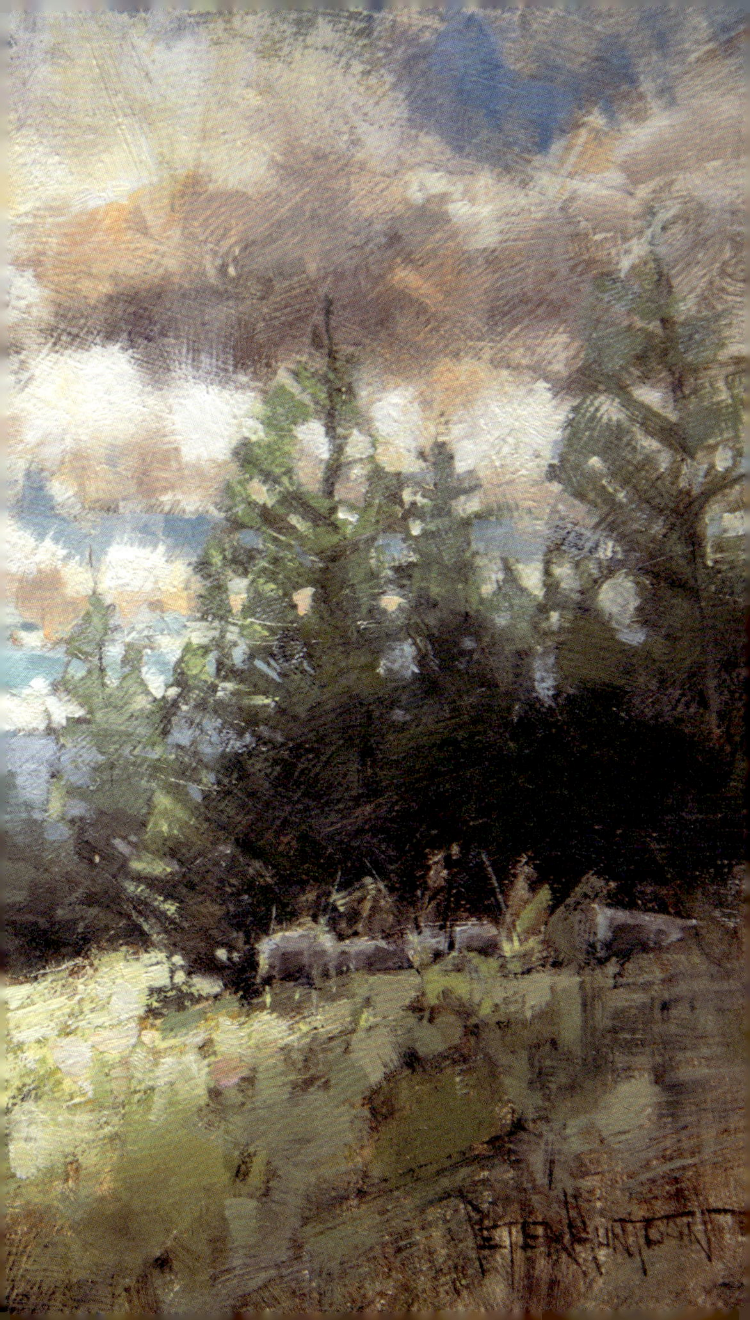

Artwork

Joseph-Antoine d'Ornano
Untitled, Cover Artwork (2020)
Ink and watercolor
8 x 6 inches

4   Sally Rosenbaum
Girl in Green Dress (2010)
Oil on canvas
24 x 36 inches

24   Edward Hopper
Railroad Sunset, detail (1929)
Oil on canvas
29 × 48 inches

54   Fritz von Wille
Taufrost, detail (n.d.)
Oil on canvas
36 x 44 inches

98   Hugo Mühlig
Musikant auf dem Heimweg (n.d.)
Gouache on card
15 x 11 inches

134   C. G. Jung
Untitled (1914–1930)
Mixed media on paper
12 x 15 inches

170   Emil Nolde
Alice (1907)
Lithograph
13 x 9 inches

192   Jackie Morris
Kingfisher (2017)
Watercolor and gold leaf
10 x 14 inches

210   Peter Huntoon
Summer Apex (2020)
Oil on panel
12 x 16 inches

Contributors

EDITORS

Jonathan Simons, Analog Sea's founding editor, is an American writer living in Germany.

Janos Tedeschi is a Swiss-Italian filmmaker and artist.

Elena Fritz is a German editor and translator.

WRITERS

David Abram is an American cultural ecologist and philosopher.

Gaston Bachelard (1884–1962) was a French philosopher whose work examines poetics and the philosophy of science.

Morris Berman is an American cultural historian and social critic.

Leonard Bernstein (1918–1990) was an American composer, conductor, pianist, and author.

Jorge Luis Borges (1899–1986) was an Argentine writer and poet.

Bertolt Brecht (1898–1956) was a German poet and playwright.

Peter Brook is an English theater director and writer based in Paris.

Maria Browning is a writer and editor living in Tennessee.

Kenneth Clark (1903–1983) was a British art historian, writer, and broadcaster.

Patrick Curry is a writer and scholar living in London.

Jonathan Davidson is a poet and writer living in Birmingham, United Kingdom.

Gretel Ehrlich is an American novelist, essayist, and poet.

Ralph Waldo Emerson (1803–1882) was an American essayist and poet.

Arthur Erickson (1924–2009) was a Canadian architect.

Anne Fadiman is an American essayist and teacher.

Howard Fink is a Canadian writer, researcher, and Professor Emeritus in English at Concordia University.

Glenn Gould (1932–1982) was a Canadian classical pianist and writer.

Alexander Graf is a writer, translator, and cinephile living in Richmond, Surrey.

Simon-Pierre Hamelin is a writer living in Tangier.

CONTRIBUTORS

Jean James is a poet, born in Northern Ireland, now living in Swansea, Wales.

Carl Gustav Jung (1875–1961) was a Swiss psychiatrist and psychoanalyst who founded analytical psychology.

Barry Lopez is an American essayist and fiction writer.

Robert Macfarlane is a British travel and nature writer.

Alberto Manguel is an Argentine-Canadian writer, translator, and editor.

Pablo Medina is a Cuban-American poet and novelist.

Jeremy Page is a poet, translator, and editor living in East Sussex, United Kingdom.

P. K. Page (1916–2010) was a Canadian poet, novelist, and artist.

Blaise Pascal (1623–1662) was a French mathematician, scientist, writer, philosopher, and theologian.

George Prochnik is a writer and independent scholar currently living in London.

Sarah Ream is an editor living in London.

Rainer Maria Rilke (1875–1926) was an Austrian poet and novelist who wrote both in German and French.

Sophy Roberts is a British journalist and author living in Dorset, England.

May Sarton (1912–1995) was a Belgian-American novelist and poet.

Ros Schwartz is a translator living in London.

Thomas R. Smith is an American poet, essayist, teacher, and editor living in Wisconsin.

Susan Sontag (1933–2004) was an American novelist, essayist, and filmmaker.

William Stafford (1914–1993) was an American poet.

Will Stone is a poet, literary translator and essayist who lives in Suffolk, England.

Harry Tomicek is an Austrian film historian and philosopher.

Jozef van der Voort is a translator and editor living in London.

Wim Wenders is a German filmmaker, author, and photographer.

Virginia Woolf (1882–1941) was an English novelist and essayist.

Stefan Zweig (1881–1942) was an Austrian biographer, essayist, novelist, and poet.

CONTRIBUTORS

INTERVIEWEES

Wolfgang Giegerich is a German psychologist, researcher, and Jungian analyst.

Andrés Ocazionez is a psychoanalyst living in Berlin.

Wim Wenders is a German filmmaker, author, and photographer.

ARTISTS

Joseph-Antoine d'Ornano is a Parisian painter and writer.

Edward Hopper (1882–1967) was an American painter from New York.

Peter Huntoon is an American painter living in Vermont.

Carl Gustav Jung (1875–1961) was a Swiss psychiatrist and psychoanalyst who founded analytical psychology.

Jackie Morris is an artist and writer who lives in Wales, by the sea.

Hugo Mühlig (1854–1929) was a German Impressionist painter.

Emil Nolde (1867–1956) was a German-Danish painter, printmaker, draftsman, and one of the first Expressionists.

Sally Rosenbaum is an artist living in California.

Fritz von Wille (1860–1941) was a German landscape painter.

Acknowledgments

5 Excerpted from "Literature Contains All Art" by Gaston Bachelard in *On Poetic Imagination and Reverie*, trans. Colette Gaudin. Copyright © 2014 by Spring Publications, Inc. Reprinted by permission of Spring Publications, Inc.

8 "Eternal Ink" by Anne Fadiman. Copyright © 1998 by Anne Fadiman. Reprinted by permission of the author. From *Ex Libris: Confessions of a Common Reader* (New York: Farrar, Straus and Giroux, 1998), pp. 87–94.

17 Excerpted from *The World of Yesterday* by Stefan Zweig, trans. Helmut Ripperger and B.W. Huebsch. Translation © 1943, 1971 by the Viking Press, Inc. Reprinted by permission of Viking Books, an imprint of Penguin Publishing Group, a division of Penguin Random House LLC.

23 "The Forging" by Jorge Luis Borges. Copyright © 2010 by Penguin Random House. Reprinted by permission of Penguin Classics, an imprint of Penguin Publishing Group, a division of Penguin Random House LLC. From *Poems of the Night*, trans. Christopher Maurer (London: Penguin Books, 2010), p. 3.

24 *Railroad Sunset* (1929) by Edward Hopper (1882–1967). Copyright © 2020 by Heirs of Josephine N. Hopper. Licensed by Artists Rights Society (ARS), NY. Photography © Whitney Museum of American Art. Licensed by Scala and Art Resource, NY. Reprinted by permission of Heirs of Josephine N. Hopper.

44 Adapted from "Alice in the Cities" by Alexander Graf in *The Cinema of Wim Wenders: The Celluloid Highway* (New York: Wallflower Press, 2002), pp. 72–91. Copyright © 2002 by Alexander Graf. Reprinted by permission of the author.

47 Excerpted from "The Old Masters: John Ford, John Ford and John Ford" by Harry Tomicek. Copyright © 2014 by Harry Tomicek. Reprinted by permission of the author. Translated by Jozef van der Voort for Analog Sea. From *Retrospektive: John Ford* (Vienna: Viennale, 2014), pp. 105–106.

49 Excerpted from "Verlorene Welt" by Siegfried Schober, first published in German in *Süddeutsche Zeitung* (September 3, 1973). Copyright © 1973 by *Süddeutsche Zeitung*. Reprinted by permission of *Süddeutsche Zeitung*.

54 *Taufrost* by Fritz von Wille. Copyright © 2014 by Van Ham Kunstauktionen and Saša Fuis Photographie.

55 Excerpted from "The Truth About a Legend" by Leonard Bernstein, first published in *Glenn Gould Variations: By Himself and His Friends*, edited with an introduction by John McGreevy (New York: Quill, 1983), pp. 17–22. Copyright © 1983 by Amberson Holdings LLC. Reprinted by permission of The Leonard Bernstein Office, Inc.

69 Excerpted from the audio transcript of "The Idea of North" by Glenn Gould. Reprinted by permission of Primary Wave, administered by

ACKNOWLEDGMENTS

CCS Rights Management Corp. From *Solitude Trilogy* (Toronto: CBC Records, 1992).

82 Excerpted from "Rotten Ice" by Gretel Ehrlich. Copyright © 2015 by *Harper's Magazine*. Excerpt reprinted from the April 2015 issue by special permission.

87 "You and Art" by William Stafford. Copyright © 1986 by University of Michigan. Reprinted by permission of University of Michigan Press. From *You Must Revise Your Life* (Ann Arbor: University of Michigan Press, 1987), p. 27.

88 Commencement address "Advice to a Graduation" by Glenn Gould, delivered at the Royal Conservatory of Music, University of Toronto, November 1964. Reprinted by permission of Primary Wave, administered by CCS Rights Management Corp.

97 "At the Blue Note" by Pablo Medina. Copyright © 2011 by Pablo Medina. Reprinted by permission of the author. From *The Man Who Wrote on Water* (Brooklyn, NY: Hanging Loose Press, 2011), p. 17.

98 *Musikant auf dem Heimweg* by Hugo Mühlig (1854–1929). Photograph © akg images. Reprinted by permission of akg images.

109 Adapted from "The English Civil War and the Nicaraguan Revolution" by Jonathan Davidson. Copyright © 2018 by Jonathan Davidson. Reprinted by permission of the author. From *On Poetry* (Sheffield: Smith|Doorstep Books, 2018), pp. 81–89.

118 "Where Are the Intellectuals?" by Alberto Manguel. Copyright © 2019 by Alberto Manguel (Schavelzon Graham Agencia Literaria). Reprinted by permission of Schavelzon Graham Agencia Literaria.

125 "In Dark Times" by Bertolt Brecht in *The Collected Poems of Bertolt Brecht*. Translation © 2019, 2015 by Tom Kuhn and David Constantine. Copyright © Bertolt-Brecht-Erben/Suhrkamp Verlag. Reprinted by permission of Liveright Publishing, a division of W. W. Norton & Company, Inc.

126 Excerpted from "The Religious Value of the Unknown" by George Prochnik in *Emergence Magazine*, no. 4. Copyright © 2019 by George Prochnik. Excerpt reprinted by permission of the author.

130 Adapted from Arthur Erickson's foreword to *Light for a Cold Land* by Peter Larisey (Toronto, ON: Dundurn Press Limited, 1993), pp. vii–ix. Copyright © 1993 by Dundurn Press Limited. Excerpt reprinted by permission of Dundurn Press Limited.

133 "This Heavy Craft" by P. K. Page in *The Hidden Room*, vol. 2 (Erin, ON: Porcupine's Quill, 1997), p. 233. Copyright © 2000 by the Estate of P.K. Page. Reprinted by permission of the Porcupine's Quill.

134 *Untitled* by C. G. Jung in *The Red Book*. Copyright © 2009 by The Foundation of the Works of C. G. Jung.

ACKNOWLEDGMENTS

Reprinted by permission of W.W. Norton & Company, Inc. From *The Red Book*, ed. Sonu Shamdasani, trans. Mark Kyburz, John Peck, and Sonu Shamdasani (London: W.W. Norton & Company Ltd., 2009), p. 131.

135 Foreword to *The Red Book* by C.G. Jung. Copyright © 2009 by The Foundation of the Works of C.G. Jung. Reprinted by permission of W.W. Norton & Company, Inc.

149 Excerpted from "The Disenchantment of the World" by Morris Berman in *The Reenchantment of the World* (Ithaca and London: Cornell University Press, 1981). Copyright © 1981 by Morris Berman. Reprinted by permission of the author.

170 *Alice* (1907) by Emil Nolde (1867–1956). Copyright © Nolde Stiftung Seebüll. Photography © The Museum of Modern Art. Licensed by Scala and Art Resource, NY. Reprinted by permission of Nolde Stiftung Seebüll.

171 Excerpted from *Journal of a Solitude* by May Sarton. Copyright © 1992 by May Sarton. Reprinted by permission of W.W. Norton & Company, Inc.

183 Excerpted from *Montaigne* by Stefan Zweig, trans. Will Stone (London: Pushkin Press, 2015). Translation © 2015 by Will Stone. Reprinted by permission of the translator.

188 Excerpted from *To the Lighthouse* by Virginia Woolf. Copyright © 1927 by Houghton Mifflin Harcourt Publishing Company, renewed 1954 by Leonard Woolf. Reprinted by permission of Houghton Mifflin Harcourt Publishing Company.

192 *Kingfisher* by Jackie Morris in *The Lost Words: A Spell Book* by Jackie Morris and Robert Macfarlane (London: Hamish Hamilton, 2017). Copyright © 2017 by Jackie Morris. Reprinted by permission of the artist.

193 Adapted from "Silt" by Robert Macfarlane in *The Old Ways: A Journey on Foot*. Copyright © 2012 by Robert Macfarlane. First published by Hamish Hamilton in 2012 and by Penguin Books in 2013. Excerpt reprinted by permission of Penguin Books Ltd and Viking Books, an imprint of Penguin Publishing Group, a division of Penguin Random House LLC.

201 "In Search of Darkness" by Maria Browning. Copyright © 2020 by Maria Browning. First published in the *New York Times* (February 23, 2020), p. 10. Reprinted by permission of the author.

206 "Newgrange" by Thomas R. Smith. Copyright © 2018 by Thomas R. Smith. Reprinted by permission of the author. From *Windy Day at Kabekona: New and Selected Poems 1978–2018* (Buffalo NY: White Pine Press, 2018).

209 "Every Morning All Over Again" by William Stafford. Copyright © 1986 by University of Michigan. Reprinted by permission of University of Michigan Press. From *You Must Revise Your Life* (Ann Arbor: University of Michigan Press, 1987), p. 38.